Whe

a Wil

Where There's a Will

BETH PATTILLO

GUIDEPOSTS
NEW YORK, NEW YORK

Where There's a Will

ISBN-13: 978-0-8249-4779-8

Published by Guideposts
16 East 34th Street
New York, New York 10016
www.guideposts.com

Distributed by Ideals Publications, a division of Guideposts
2636 Elm Hill Pike, Suite 120
Nashville, Tennessee 37214

Library of Congress Cataloging-in-Publication Data

Pattillo, Beth.
  Where there's a will / Beth Pattillo.
      p. cm.—(Mystery and the minister's wife)
  ISBN 978-0-8249-4779-8
  1. Spouses of clergy—Fiction. 2. Clergy—Fiction. 3. Inheritance and succession—Fiction. 4. Land titles—Fiction. 5. Wills—Fiction. I. Title.
  PS3616.A925W47 2009
  813'.6--dc22
                                                  2009008222

Cover by Lookout Design Group
Interior design by Cris Kossow
Typeset by Nancy Tardi

Printed and bound in the United States of America

10 9 8 7 6 5 4 3 2 1

For Harvey C. Smith and Mary Lou Smith,
my wonderful in-laws.
Thank you for your love and support.

Chapter One

Kate Hanlon checked the number posted above the classroom doorway against the number written on the slip of paper in her hand. She'd followed the campus map of Pine Ridge College to the right building, but finding the correct classroom had proved more daunting.

Room 203.

Yes, that was it. She took a deep breath and stepped inside. The tile floor, venetian blinds, and slightly musty smell were familiar to any student, but a few things had changed in the decades since Kate had stepped foot in a college classroom. A large television was mounted near the ceiling in one corner, and an LCD projector sat on a cabinet in the middle of the room. Kate looked around the room with excitement. Judging from the rows and rows of empty desks, she was earlier than she'd thought.

"Good morning!" A dark-haired woman about Kate's age stepped from behind a desk at the front of the classroom. "I'm Professor Carruthers. And you are, as you can see"—she waved a hand toward the empty classroom as she smiled—"the first to arrive."

Although Kate was a mature adult, her early arrival still made her feel like a lost freshman on the first day of classes. Somehow she found returning to school in her late fifties far more intimidating than it had been the first time around.

"I'm Kate Hanlon." She smiled to hide her nerves and extended her hand, expecting the professor to take it. Instead, an odd expression crossed the woman's face.

"Oh, I see."

A knot tightened in Kate's stomach. That was certainly not the reaction she had been expecting from her new professor. She'd enrolled in the art history course at the college with a great deal of trepidation. A lifetime devoted to children, work, a loving husband, and church hadn't left much time for continued study. But her passion for stained glass had inspired her to return to school. If she was to grow as an artist, furthering her knowledge of art history seemed a logical step.

"Am I in the wrong class?" Kate took a nervous step backward.

The other woman's clouded expression cleared, and her smile returned. "No, no, not at all. I'm sorry. Normally I have much better manners. It's just that—"

The professor stopped speaking and looked toward the doorway. Kate turned to see two familiar faces from Copper Mill.

"Martha? Dot?" Kate said in surprise.

Martha Sinclair and Dot Bagley were members of Faith Briar Church, where Kate's husband, Paul, was the pastor. They were also regulars at Betty's Beauty Parlor and two of the more active branches on the Copper Mill grapevine. Kate often visited with them while she was having her hair done, but she never dreamed of encountering the two women in an art history class. They had always seemed more interested in gossip than fine arts.

"Are you two taking this class?" Kate asked, careful to hide her disbelief.

"Well, when we heard you talking about it at the beauty shop, it sounded so interesting," Martha said with her usual wide smile, "that we thought we'd give it a try."

Kate bit back a sigh. She was very fond of the people at Faith Briar, but ministers' wives sometimes needed a little time away from their congregations. She had hoped to find some space at the college, but apparently that wasn't going to happen.

"I didn't know you were interested in nineteenth-century American art," Kate said.

"We love all those pretty pictures," Martha gushed.

Out of the corner of her eye, Kate saw Professor Carruthers blanch.

"I think you'll find we will be concerned with far more than *pretty pictures*, as you say." The professor's tone was curt. "Why don't you take your seats? I'm sure the remainder of the class will arrive in a moment."

Martha and Dot appeared unperturbed by the woman's abruptness, and they happily set about the business of selecting their desks. Kate followed them, but she would have preferred to continue her conversation with Professor Carruthers. Why had the woman reacted so strangely when Kate introduced herself? As a pastor's wife, she had grown accustomed to occasional frowns of disapproval, but she usually knew the reasons behind them. The professor's reaction, along with Martha and Dot's appearance, drained away a significant portion of Kate's anticipation of the class.

Fortunately, the other students began to arrive. Most of them were young—quite young, it seemed to Kate, who felt every one of her fifty-seven years as she watched them file into the room. Their choppy hairstyles, unique piercings, backpacks, and tight blouses over low-waisted pants heightened her awareness of her ordinary strawberry blonde curls and sweater set. She enjoyed keeping up with fashion and wore stylish clothes, but that didn't stop her from feeling more like a mother than a peer in the company of her fellow students.

At last, the classroom filled, the students took their seats, and the bell tower chimed to announce the hour.

Professor Carruthers stood and introduced herself, gave an overview of the course, and discussed the syllabus. Then she dimmed the lights. A breathtaking image filled the screen at the front of the classroom. Kate recognized the masterpiece as *Whistler's Mother*. A warm feeling of relief and pleasure washed over her, sweeping away her discomfort. She'd chosen to study nineteenth-century American art because the realism and strong use of color spoke to her own creative sensibilities. She hoped to capture that same striking visual imagery in her own work someday.

The ninety-minute class passed in the blink of an eye, or at least it seemed that way to Kate. When Professor

Carruthers flipped the lights back on, Kate blinked against the harsh fluorescent glare. Before dismissing the group, the professor gave them their assignment for the next class—a great deal of reading as well as a paper that would require viewing a number of slides at the library.

Kate sat motionless for a long moment as the other students rose from their desks and filed past her. She studied the syllabus, noting that the assignments didn't get any easier as the semester progressed, especially when she read the description of the final project. As much as the subject matter excited Kate, she wondered if she'd bitten off more than she could chew.

"Kate? Could I speak to you for a moment?"

The professor's question startled her.

"Oh . . . why, yes, of course." Kate scrambled for her handbag and the notebook she'd brought. All of the students, except for Kate, Martha, and Dot, had laptop computers. Kate stood and made her way up the aisle between the desks.

As Kate approached the front of the room, she could feel her pulse pick up. She was certain she was about to be told that she didn't belong in the class.

She was so nervous that she almost didn't notice the forced smile on the professor's face or the white-knuckled hands that were holding several pages of lecture notes.

"I have to apologize," Professor Carruthers began, not quite meeting Kate's eyes. "I didn't mean to react so strangely when you introduced yourself. It's just that you're the last person I ever expected to have in one of my classes."

Kate put on a brave smile of her own. She had been right. The professor didn't think she belonged in the class. Of course, her undergraduate degree hadn't been in fine arts, but the college registrar had assured her she didn't need any prerequisites for the class.

"I understand," Kate said before the professor could continue. "Thank you, though, for letting me sit in on today's lecture. It was worth it just for the overview—"

"Oh no. You don't understand." Professor Carruthers' eyes widened in alarm. "This has nothing to do with you as a student."

"It doesn't?" Kate was baffled. *Then what on earth?* she wondered.

"You're Paul Hanlon's wife, aren't you?" she asked. "The one who solves mysteries?"

Now Kate was more confused than ever. "Yes . . . Yes, I am."

Professor Carruthers dropped her lecture notes on the desk and sighed. "I'm afraid I'm making a terrible mess of this." She paused and took a deep breath. "My maiden name is Harrington. I'm Ellen Harrington."

Kate stared at the woman and tried to keep her jaw from dropping. "Paul's Ellen Harrington?"

"I'm afraid so," Ellen answered with a modest smile.

As surprised as the woman had apparently been to have Kate as a student, Kate had equally never anticipated having her husband's old girlfriend as a professor.

"I thought you lived in upstate New York," Kate said.

Bits of information pushed to the forefront of her

mind. Paul and Ellen had met during their freshman year at East Tennessee State University. The pair of them had been pretty serious according to Paul's mother, who had never quite forgiven Kate for being a Texas native rather than a homegrown Tennessee girl. Kate had never been clear on exactly why Paul and Ellen had parted ways, but their romance hadn't survived past graduation.

Ellen Carruthers' smile disappeared. "I did live in New York until a few weeks ago." Her eyes misted over. "You see, I lost my husband, Trevor, last spring."

Sympathy quickly alleviated any dawning pangs of jealousy Kate felt. "I'm so sorry. I had no idea."

"No, of course you wouldn't." Ellen gave her a weak smile. "Paul and I lost touch long ago after I moved to Boston for graduate school." A shadow crossed her face.

Kate and Ellen exchanged a bittersweet look of understanding.

"But I actually didn't ask you to stay behind because of Paul," Ellen said. "I've heard you have a certain reputation for solving people's problems, and I have one I could use your help with."

Kate braced herself. Ever since she'd had some success solving the mysteries around Copper Mill, she'd begun receiving all sorts of requests for help. For the most part, they were fairly innocuous and didn't require more than ordinary common sense to figure out. Lost keys could be located by retracing a person's steps. Long-lost relatives took a little more time to find, but they usually turned up with a thorough Google search on the computer at the

Copper Mill Public Library. But every so often, a full-fledged, bona fide mystery presented itself, and Kate's curiosity always got the better of her.

"A problem so soon after moving back to the area?" Kate asked.

With any luck, Ellen Carruthers' difficulty would be a minor one, easily resolved. While Kate would naturally have been hesitant about taking on a mystery for her new professor, the fact that the woman was Paul's former girlfriend made it doubly tricky.

"Actually," Ellen said, "this particular mystery has been brewing for two generations."

Kate's interest was piqued despite her reservations. "Really?" Surely Ellen was exaggerating.

"I need help finding my Grandfather Harrington's second will. I don't know if Paul ever mentioned it, but my family is the original Harrington clan for whom this county is named. Finding the will is the only way I can assert my claim to part interest in a rather large piece of property."

Now Kate was more than interested. She was downright intrigued. "How long has the will been missing?"

Ellen shook her head. "I'm not sure. You see, I've never actually seen the will, although I know it exists."

"You haven't tried to find the will before now?"

Ellen grimaced. "Honestly, I hoped I would never need to bother with it at all. My cousin Carol Coats is the majority owner of the property, and her husband Oliver has been very unpleasant about the whole matter, so much so that I never pursued my claim. For years no one had any interest in the property, including me, so it didn't matter. In fact, if I'd known what would happen, I might not have come home at all. But last month some people from the state government approached Oliver about buying the land. They want to turn it into a wildlife preserve."

"How did you find out about the offer?"

"Carol and I do talk occasionally, when Oliver's not around."

"And where is the property?" Kate asked.

"Have you ever heard of High Hoot Ridge?"

"Where the old Harrington Ironworks are?"

"Yes."

Kate had indeed heard of it. The abandoned mining town of Harrington and its ironworks were something of a local legend, a ghost town on a ridge east of Copper Mill.

"And your family owned it?"

"My great-grandfather and his brother were the original owners. In fact, both the town and the county were named after them. But the two brothers had a falling out, and the town was abandoned in the early 1900s. The land's just been sitting there ever since, passed down through the family."

"And selling it to the government won't settle the dispute? Your cousin wouldn't consider simply handing over your fair share?"

"Oliver would never let her, not when I can't show proof of my claim to the property. My grandfather's first will was written before I was born, and it left his share of the property to Carol, with only a life interest for my grandmother. There are some other cousins who also have a minor interest in the property, but Carol or, more accurately, Oliver controls both her grandfather's share and mine."

"How do you know the second will exists?" Kate had seen on more than one occasion that people's hopes often didn't reflect reality. She would hate to go on a wild-goose chase for a nonexistent document.

"My grandmother never told me about the will while she was alive," Ellen said. "But after her death almost thirty years ago, I received a letter from her telling me the truth. She knew I wanted to stay out of the family squabbles, but she also wanted me to have the opportunity to claim my inheritance if I ever changed my mind. She didn't trust Carol's father, her nephew, so she hid the will . . . very, very well."

"And no one's uncovered it in all this time?"

"As I said, I was willing to let a sleeping dog lie. If nothing else, I've learned over the years that family fights about money never produce winners—only losers." Ellen paused, then went on. "You see, my parents died when I was quite young, and I was raised by my grandparents. The land was their only legacy to me. Now, with Trevor's death and this offer from the state to buy the property, it's become more important than ever that I find the will. Financially, if not just for my own peace of mind. So, do you think you can help me?"

Kate hesitated. "Do you have any idea where it might be?"

Ellen smiled. "Yes. And I think you'll find this interesting. You see, it's something of an art history puzzle."

"What do you mean?"

"My grandmother was an artist. She was the one who nurtured my love of painting. So when she hid the will, she left clues. She counted on my love of art to help me solve the mystery."

Kate smiled. "You're right. I'm definitely intrigued. Tell me more."

"She created a series of paintings that would lead me to the will."

"If she left such a clear trail, why do you need my help?"

"That's just it." Ellen frowned. "There's nothing clear about any of it. First of all, I have only one of the five paintings needed to solve the mystery. The rest were dispersed among various family members."

Ellen was right. Kate was beginning to find the mystery irresistible. "Do the other family members know that the paintings are clues to the whereabouts of the will?"

"No. Grandmother only revealed the secret to me in the letter, and I've never mentioned it to anyone."

"So you need me to help you find the paintings?" Perhaps it wouldn't be much more difficult than finding lost keys, she thought. One simply needed to trace the whereabouts of the paintings' owners.

"Yes," Ellen answered. "If you can help me locate all of them, I believe we can solve the puzzle and find the will."

"And if we succeed, do I get an A in your class?" Kate asked with a chuckle.

Ellen laughed, and her shoulders sagged with relief. "Then you'll help me?"

"If you'll let me stay in the class," Kate said. "I was

afraid you were going to tell me I didn't belong here with all these young students."

"Oh, there's no question about your place in this class." Ellen gave Kate a reassuring smile. "Besides, it's nice to have someone my own age around."

Kate breathed a sigh of relief. "So, where do we start our search?"

"With my cousin Carol. Well, actually, with her husband, Oliver. They have at least one of the paintings that I'm aware of."

"If you'll call him and set up an appointment, we can pay him a visit and get started." Kate mentally reviewed her schedule, trying to recall her various commitments over the next few days.

"Um . . . well . . ." Ellen hesitated. "There might be one small problem with that."

"What problem?" She studied Ellen's worried expression with misgiving.

Ellen crossed her arms. "Oliver would never agree to a meeting with me. He thinks I'm a bad influence on Carol."

"So you want me to go see him on your behalf?" Kate was immediately wary.

"He'd never turn away a preacher's wife. He's too conscious of his standing in the community."

Kate paused. She didn't like to get involved in family conflicts, but she also wanted to help Ellen.

"Let me think about it," she said. "I do want to help, but just because I've had some luck in the past doesn't mean I can locate the paintings. You might get your hopes up for nothing."

"If you'd just try to talk to him, I'd really appreciate it."

"I'll give it some thought."

"Why don't you come to my apartment for tea tomorrow?" Ellen asked. "I can show you my painting, maybe persuade you to help me."

Kate smiled with reluctant agreement. "All right. That would be fine."

Kate waited while Ellen gathered up her things, and the two women left the classroom together. They parted ways outside the building, and Kate walked through the beautiful campus toward the parking lot where she'd left her car.

Why was it that everywhere she went, mysteries always seemed to find her? Paul often preached about finding your God-given gifts and using them. At first, Kate hadn't thought of her amateur detective work as a gift, but from other people's perspectives, perhaps it was. If so, then she had a responsibility to use it to help others.

How ironic that her professor had turned out to be Paul's former girlfriend. Kate wasn't worried about Ellen's reappearance in their lives, but if she didn't feel the tiniest bit odd about Ellen's previous relationship with Paul, well, then she'd hardly have been female, would she?

Kate chuckled to herself as she climbed in the car and turned on the radio to find some music for the ride home.

Chapter Two

That night after dinner, Kate and Paul retired to the living room. Paul started a cozy blaze in the fireplace, then settled on the sofa next to Kate and picked up that day's issue of the *Copper Mill Chronicle*.

"How did your first class go this morning?" he asked.

Kate was thankful for the support Paul had shown when she'd told him of her desire to go back to school. He'd shown her that same support and encouragement in her stained glass work.

"Well, it was . . . um . . . interesting. Definitely interesting."

"How so?" Paul asked, looking up from his newspaper.

"Well, my professor is someone you know," Kate had to hide her smile.

"Really? Who?"

"Ellen Harrington. Or Professor Ellen Carruthers, as she's now known." She waited to see Paul's reaction.

He blinked. "Ellen? Really?"

Kate studied his face carefully. Of course, she was secure in her marriage to Paul. They'd been a happy couple for almost thirty years now. Still, it was disconcerting to any woman when one of her husband's former girlfriends turned up. Especially when that girlfriend was of the "first love" variety.

"Yes, really. And I was surprised, to say the least."

A smile spread across Paul's face. "Wow! It would be great to see her again. I've always been sorry we lost touch."

For a moment, he appeared lost in thought, and Kate felt the teensiest bit of anxiety.

"How's she doing?" he asked. "I wonder what brought her back to Tennessee."

"Actually, she lost her husband last spring." Kate felt another wave of sympathy for Ellen. She couldn't imagine going on with her life without Paul, and from what she could tell, Ellen had felt the same way about her late husband.

Paul's expression sobered. "That's too bad. We should make her feel welcome, invite her to dinner, maybe."

"She also had a request for me."

"What kind?" Then he sighed. "Don't tell me. Another mystery for the minister's wife to solve?"

Kate smiled. Paul had shown great forbearance with all of her sleuthing since they'd moved to Copper Mill. A handy quality in a husband that she had long ago learned to appreciate.

"So what's the mystery?" Paul asked.

Kate explained Ellen's story, and what she had asked Kate to do. "It sounds like she really needs some help, and maybe even a friend."

Paul reached over and kissed her on the cheek. "That's my Katie. Not many women would volunteer to help out their husband's old flame." His teasing grin and the loving light in his eyes warmed her heart. Like any married couple, she and Paul had experienced their ups and downs. But at the end of the day, they were always delighted to come home to each other.

"Well, I happen to be quite extraordinary, in case it escaped your notice," Kate replied saucily.

"Katie, nothing about you has ever escaped my notice," he said, reaching for her. She giggled when Paul pulled her closer and proceeded to demonstrate just how extraordinary he found her.

Sometimes mysteries, and even former girlfriends, needed to take a backseat to old-fashioned love and affection.

THE NEXT AFTERNOON, Paul entered the Country Diner with more trepidation than he'd felt since he and Kate made the move to Copper Mill. True, they had adjusted to small-town life pretty well, just as the folks of Copper Mill had adjusted to a "citified" preacher and his cosmopolitan wife. But when Lawton Briddle, the mayor of Copper Mill, had called Paul the previous week and invited him to join the Copper Mill Chamber of Commerce, Paul had immediately felt his pulse shift into overdrive.

Try as he might, he couldn't think of a single reason for the mayor to extend such an invitation. The chamber was for businessmen, not clergymen. What's more, it had always been limited to an exclusive handful of old-timers, not transplants like himself. Still, Paul had been in Copper Mill long enough not only to gain some insight into the little community but also to form some opinions about its future. What better place to advocate for much-needed changes than within the inner circle of the town's movers and shakers?

"Rev. Hanlon. We're glad you could make it." As mayor, Lawton presided over the official Copper Mill Chamber of Commerce from his seat at the back corner booth. Three other men sat in a semicircle around him: Fred Cowan, the owner of the pharmacy across from Willy's Bait and Tackle; Clifton Beasley, a regular among the retired men who drank coffee on the porch of the local mercantile; and John Sharpe, the town's only insurance agent. Paul greeted each one in turn and shook hands.

"Sit down, sit down," Lawton said. "We'll get started just as soon as LuAnne brings us our pie. Ah, here she comes."

LuAnne Matthews was as much a fixture of the Country Diner as the strong coffee and biscuits and gravy. The red-haired waitress handed the plates around the table, then fixed her lively green eyes on Paul.

"Afternoon, Preacher," she said with a smile and a wink. "What'll it be today? A little something to clog your arteries?"

One aspect of small-town life that Paul thoroughly enjoyed was that cholesterol took a backseat to good country cooking.

"Pecan pie, warmed, with vanilla ice cream and black coffee, please," he said with a grin. He kept to a fairly healthy diet, under Kate's watchful eye, but how could anyone be expected to drink a cup of coffee at the diner and not enjoy the mouthwatering taste of the baked goods every now and then?

The men talked about the warm fall weather and the prospects of the Copper Mill High School football team until LuAnne returned with Paul's order, then the mayor officially began the meeting by tapping on the table with a spoon.

"Gentlemen, our first order of business is to welcome Rev. Hanlon, which I think we've already done." The other men nodded in agreement. "So, our next item on the agenda is to decide whose wife is going to be in charge of the Christmas Craft Extravaganza."

Paul took a sip of his coffee as the other men issued a collective groan.

"My wife was in charge last year," Clifton said. "So I'm off the hook." He sighed. "That cost me a trip to Nashville. Near about killed my back toting around all those shopping bags."

The other men made sympathetic noises, but no one volunteered to be the one to approach their spouse. Paul swallowed. If he was going to gain any credibility with the group, he'd have to step up.

"I suppose I could talk to Kate about it," he began.

The other men perked up immediately.

"Good," said Lawton. "Then that's taken care of."

Paul held up a hand. While he was willing to step up, he wasn't so sure how Kate might feel about heading up such an event. "I said I'd ask Kate, but I can't promise anything. She has her hands pretty full these days."

"But she doesn't work," Clifton said. "What else does she have to do with her time?"

Paul held his tongue. The question was ironic coming from Clifton, who spent most days in a rocking chair on the porch of Sam Gorman's Mercantile, drinking coffee and spinning yarns with the other retired men of Copper Mill.

Lawton cleared his throat. "The next item on the list is trickier."

"Don't tell me Emma's complaining about us again," Clifton said, referring to the proprietor of Emma's Ice Cream Shop, the business adjacent to the Mercantile. "We're not hurting her business just by hangin' around next door."

"No, no." Lawton raised a hand. "That Luke Danvers fellow from the state community development office wants to meet with us again."

Paul leaned forward. Now this was more what he'd been expecting when he'd accepted the mayor's invitation to join the chamber. Perhaps someone from the development office could help with the pressing need for more jobs in the area. Communities often failed to take advantage of such resources.

Clifton snorted. "He's like a dog with a bone, that man. What's he lathered up about now?"

The mayor frowned. "Now, Clifton, we don't want to give Rev. Hanlon here the wrong impression. With the way you're talking, he's going to think we're against progress in Copper Mill."

"We're against ruining this community," Clifton protested, swirling the remains of the coffee in his cup.

"We don't want a SuperMart like the one in Pine Ridge. Our stores struggle enough just to stay open as it is."

Fred Cowan nodded in agreement. "If one of those chain pharmacies comes here, I'll be out of business within a year."

John Sharpe looked thoughtful. "We're going to have to broaden our tax base somehow. This town hasn't been the same since the copper mines shut down back in the seventies."

Paul looked from one man to the other, keenly aware of the mixed feelings around the table. These men were seeing the only way of life they'd loved and known slowly disappearing. As John had observed, the economic decline in Copper Mill had been going on for decades ever since the mining industry had gone bust. Copper Mill wasn't in any immediate danger of collapse, but groups like the chamber of commerce needed to look to the future now more than ever.

"How long has it been since you met with this fellow?" Paul asked.

Clifton shrugged. "Five, maybe six years. The only thing he wanted to do was talk about bringing in outsiders."

The mayor nodded. "We're agreed that what we want to do is develop local businesses, not get taken over by some big corporation."

The other men murmured their assent. Paul hesitated. As the newest member of the chamber, he'd planned to simply sit and listen during his first meeting. But five or six years? Surely it was well past time to talk with the community development man again.

"Would it hurt just to hear this Danvers fellow out?" Paul asked. "He might have some fresh ideas."

John shook his head. "Waste of time. We're better off just keeping on doing what we're doing. Slow and steady wins the race. Right, Pastor?"

What could he say? Paul sipped his coffee to stall for time. He'd grown up only an hour from Copper Mill, so he knew how insular a small town could be, how outsiders were viewed with caution at best and suspicion at worst. His Tennessee roots were probably the only reason Lawton had invited him to join the group.

Paul paused. "I wonder, though, if you could develop any kind of new business, what kind of growth would you like to see in Copper Mill?"

The other men frowned, perplexed.

Finally, Fred replied. "I'd like to see small stores. Mom-and-pop businesses. That's what will help us preserve our town. People need a stake, not just a paycheck."

"Then why not talk to the man from the state office about that?" Paul urged, treading carefully.

"I don't see any point in that," Lawton said, delivering the proclamation with his usual air of authority. "We're just going to have to figure this out ourselves."

Paul sighed and took another sip of his coffee. He knew it would be an uphill battle to convince these old-timers to listen to any new ideas, but he wasn't ready to give up just yet. No, he was just getting started in fact. He stared at the empty plate sitting in front of him and thought perhaps he ought to order a second piece of pie to give him strength for the climb.

PAUL LEFT THE chamber of commerce meeting an hour later, full of pie and coffee but not as full of optimism about Copper Mill's future. He walked across the Town Square to the Mid-Cumberland Bank and Trust to make a deposit, but before he reached the door, he spotted Mike Rowland, a member of Faith Briar Church, coming down the sidewalk.

"Afternoon, Preacher." Mike extended his hand, and Paul shook it.

"Good to see you, Mike. It's been a while." Paul looked at the young man who had left Copper Mill six months earlier in search of work. Mike seemed to have aged several years in the time he'd been gone. "We've missed you. What brings you back home?"

Mike shrugged, and his gaze dropped. "Layoffs at the plant in Nashville. You know how it goes. Last hired, first fired. So I'm back here in Copper Mill until I find something else."

Paul put a hand on the young man's shoulder. Mike was in his early twenties, and though he'd done well in high school, his family didn't have the money to send him to college. With a limited number of decent-paying jobs in Copper Mill, Mike had gone off to the big city to try to make his way in the world.

"I'm sorry to hear that. You living at your folks' place?"

"Yeah, but only until I can find work. It's pretty crowded at home." Mike was the oldest of six children, the youngest still in junior high school. "I've got a friend in Chattanooga who says they're hiring in construction, so I'm going to try my luck down there."

Paul nodded but kept his expression neutral. The young man's words pained him. Mike was just one example of the late-teen and twentysomething Copper Mill natives who hadn't been able to carve out a future in their own hometown.

"Can the church do anything to help?" Paul asked, knowing even as he spoke the words that Mike would turn down his offer. Folks in Copper Mill were as proud as they were generous, which meant they always wanted to help out but often found it hard to accept it themselves.

"Well, I guess you could ask folks to pray for me." Mike brushed his longish brown hair out of his eyes. "I know the Lord must have a plan for me, but I wish it would lead me back here for good. It's hard to leave home."

"I know your folks have missed you," Paul added. "A lot of us have."

Young men like Mike were a real asset to a small community. Not only were they the ones who coached Little League teams and taught Sunday school, but they were also the town's future leaders.

A shadow passed over Mike's face. "I know, Pastor. I wish I didn't have to leave again, but I don't know what else to do."

"I understand, Mike."

The two said good-bye, and Paul continued on his way to the bank, feeling even more burdened than he had when he left the diner. His conversation with Mike made his first encounter with the chamber of commerce doubly frustrating. By wearing blinders when it came to community growth, Lawton and his cronies could fill up their time with busywork like the Christmas Craft Extravaganza and the Men's Golf Scramble without ever addressing the deeper needs of the town.

Paul slipped inside the bank, still lost in thought.

"Hello, Rev. Hanlon." Melvin McKinney appeared at Paul's side. The bank manager sported his ever-present bow tie and horn-rimmed glasses. "How can we help you today?"

Paul looked around the bank. These days, the only employees were Melvin; Matt Lawson, who was an investment adviser; and Evelyn and Georgia Cline, elderly twin sisters who had been tellers at the bank for as long as anyone could remember.

"Just making a deposit," Paul said. He nodded toward the empty cubicles where the loan manager and other employees had once worked. "A lot of empty chairs these days."

Melvin sighed and nodded. "Isn't the same, is it?" he said. "Seems that everyone's gone off to Nashville or one of the other cities to find work."

"Not always by choice, though," Paul replied.

"True." Melvin slipped off his glasses and proceeded to clean them with a handkerchief he drew out of his pocket. "The town's economy never recovered after the copper mines shut down," he said, echoing what John Sharpe had told Paul earlier that afternoon. Melvin put his glasses back on, then with one finger pushed them higher on the bridge of his nose. "I don't guess it ever will."

Paul knew that Copper Mill's problems weren't unique. Small towns all across the country struggled with the same dilemma.

"What do you think it would take to bring the town back, Melvin?" If anyone knew the answer to that question, it would be the manager of the local bank. He had to be more familiar with the business aspect of the community than anyone. Paul wondered why Melvin had never been asked to serve on the chamber of commerce.

The bank manager shrugged. "There's no primary industry, like it used to be when the mining company was the biggest employer. Some small towns grow their economies the hard way, one step at a time." He paused. "Or else they lure manufacturers by giving tax incentives they can't afford. Or they sweeten the pot with other things."

"Other things?"

Melvin looked Paul in the eye. "Bribes, plain and simple. That's one way to do it." He started to take off his glasses as if he meant to clean them again, and then he stopped. "Or there's the third way."

"Which is?"

"To stick your head in the sand and hope the problem will solve itself."

Melvin didn't have to say any more. Paul knew he was referring to the mayor and the men who ran the town, men like Fred Cowan and John Sharpe.

"I was curious why more businesses in town aren't members of the chamber of commerce," Paul ventured.

"Not much point. The bank pays in every year, so technically we belong, but I've got better things to do with my time than shoot the breeze over coffee at the diner."

"*Hmm.*" Paul didn't want to say anything against the

members of the chamber, so he smiled and said, "Guess I'd better make my deposit and get back to the church. I appreciate your insights, Melvin."

The bank manager chuckled. "Well, you're welcome, I guess. Not sure my insights, as you call them, are worth much around here."

Paul patted him on the shoulder, then crossed to the counter where Evelyn and Georgia, veteran bank employees, sat perched on high stools on the other side. "Afternoon, ladies. You're both looking lovely today."

The sisters giggled. "What can we help you with, Rev. Hanlon?" they asked almost in unison.

Georgia Cline took care of Paul's deposit and handed him a slip. He bid the twins a good day, waved at Melvin as he crossed the lobby, and walked out into the September sunshine.

Small towns had so much to offer. A sense of community, a slower pace. But they also had their challenges. As Paul walked toward his pickup truck, he wondered how he could possibly help turn around an economy that had been struggling for such a long time. Perhaps with a little faith and a lot of prayer, an opportunity might present itself.

Paul certainly hoped so. As delicious as the pies were at the Country Diner and as often as he anticipated enjoying them at future chamber of commerce meetings, he was determined to contribute more to his community than those pies would add to his waistline.

Chapter Three

That same afternoon, Kate sat on Ellen Carruthers' sofa in her small faculty apartment at the college. The living room had a minimal amount of space, but Ellen had excellent taste, and her home was both beautiful and gracious.

"I appreciate this so much," Ellen said as she offered Kate a plate of butter cookies. "Your help could make all the difference."

Kate took a cookie and set it on the tea saucer she was balancing on her knee. The cookies looked so delicious, she would have liked to have taken more than one, but she had gained a few extra pounds lately and was trying to eat more sensibly. The fact that she often liked to bake while puzzling out one of her mysteries wasn't helping her waistline any.

"I'll do my best," Kate said, "but I can't promise anything." She took a bite of her cookie, then tucked it back on the edge of her saucer. "Your grandfather's will might be long gone by now. I don't want to give you false hope."

"I have faith in my grandmother," Ellen said, taking a small sip of her tea. "She would never be careless with my legacy." Her brow furrowed. "Not as careless as I've been about looking for that will at any rate."

"I'd love to know more about the paintings," Kate suggested. "If you'd like to show me the first one . . ." She let the suggestion trail off.

Ellen seemed to collect herself. She set her cup and saucer on a small table next to her wingback chair and stood.

"Of course. If you'll just follow me."

Ellen led Kate from the tiny living room into the even smaller bedroom beyond. As in the living room, the walls were covered with paintings, collages, and sketches. Ellen's collection was truly impressive. But it was the painting above the bed that caught Kate's eye.

It looked as if a child had painted it, but as Kate stepped closer, she realized it wasn't what it appeared to be at first glance.

"Your grandmother was a Primitive painter?" she asked with surprise. Definitely not what she'd been expecting.

Ellen moved to stand beside her. "She had a lot in common with Grandma Moses," she replied, referring to the well-known American Primitive artist. "Folk art began to move into the mainstream in the early twentieth century. Of course, my grandmother painted these long after that."

Kate nodded as she admired the artist's use of color and line. The picture was deceptively simple. It showed a clearing on a ridge, surrounded by trees. A large yellow sun shone down from the sky. Here and there, a shy deer or squirrel peeped out from behind a bush or tree trunk. Under one particular tree, apples lay strewn about, nature's bounty having fallen with no one but the animals to enjoy it.

"Is this a real place?" Kate asked. Even in its artistic simplicity, the painting conveyed a strong sense of peace, giving the landscape a feeling of holiness.

"That's High Hoot Ridge," Ellen answered. "Where the Harrington family ironworks were located. The town of Harrington is a quarter mile farther along the ridge."

"Your grandmother painted this landscape from memory?"

"No. The ironworks were there long before she was born. She must have simply imagined how it looked before man came along to stake his claim."

Kate nodded. The painting certainly resonated with her because she longed to capture exactly that feeling in her own stained glass work—that sense of something more meaningful than human beings or even the natural world, but captured in a simple, austere style. "She was a very talented artist."

"Thank you." Ellen gazed at the painting a moment longer, then turned toward Kate and sighed. "If only I had half of her ability."

"You're a painter?"

Ellen laughed, the sound tinged with self-deprecation and acceptance. "No, unfortunately. I might pick up a brush now and then, but it's only for my own enjoyment." Her eyes darkened as if she was lost in memory, and then they cleared once more. "No, I'm definitely an art historian, not an artist."

Kate smiled sympathetically. "I took some art classes in college, but I didn't have enough talent to justify a degree. Not when it came to painting anyway."

"So why are you taking my class?"

"I found another outlet for my creative impulses." Kate hesitated. Sometimes when she told people that she worked with stained glass, they looked at her strangely.

"Which is?" Ellen looked intrigued.

"Stained glass, actually."

"Oh . . . sun catchers and that sort of thing?"

"Yes, but I also made a window for our church sanctuary, and I sell some of my work at Smith Street Gifts."

A light of respect flickered in Ellen's eyes, and Kate turned back to the painting, pleased at Ellen's approval. Even at her age, she still wanted the teacher to like her. "So, what kind of clue do you think your grandmother's painting gives about the will?"

Ellen sank down on the bed, turning her gaze back to the painting. She shrugged. "I've studied this picture for hours on end, and I still have no idea what it's meant to tell me."

"Did your grandmother ever talk to you about this painting?" Surely she had given Ellen some information.

Ellen shook her head. "Not specifically. Not that I remember." She plucked at the bedspread and smoothed out the creases she had made. "I should have paid more attention, I guess. All I know is that there are five paintings meant to lead me to the will."

Kate moved around the side of the bed to study the painting in closer detail. "Is there anything unusual in this one? Anything that would be out of place maybe? Or wrong for the scene?"

"Not that I can tell. She's captured the line of the ridge perfectly. I think it's a wonderfully realistic depiction of what it could have looked like before the ironworks were built."

Up close, Kate could indeed appreciate the artist's attention to detail. Though painters in the American Primitive style were often dismissed as folk artists, one couldn't deny on closer inspection the mastery of technique necessary to turn such simplicity into something so extraordinary.

"Do you have a magnifying glass?" Kate asked. "Perhaps the clue is so small that it's undetectable to the naked eye."

"I have one somewhere around here. Just a moment, and I'll see if I can find it."

Ellen left the room in search of the requested item. Kate studied the painting a while longer, then she gave up with a sigh. If there was some sort of clue in this ordinary landscape, she certainly couldn't see it.

While Kate waited for Ellen to return, she began to look idly around the room. The bed took up most of the space, but a tall chest of drawers occupied one corner, and a set of bookshelves, filled to overflowing, occupied the wall opposite the bed.

She wandered over to the chest to look at the photographs arranged on top. A number of frames—some new, others obviously from further back in Ellen's history—took up most of the space. In one of the photos, Ellen wore a wedding gown and was standing beside a thin, pleasant-looking man in a tuxedo. There were other photos of a younger Ellen in graduation gowns. Several shots showed Ellen with people Kate assumed to be colleagues from her teaching days. And then Kate saw a familiar face in a photo at the back. It showed a smiling Ellen pressed against the side of a young man who was obviously delighted to have his arm around the pretty girl. And that young man was none other than Paul Hanlon.

At that moment, Ellen returned. "Here it is. Sorry it took me so long to—" She stopped short.

Kate froze as if she'd been caught going through Ellen's drawers rather than merely looking at a few photographs.

"I didn't mean to snoop," Kate said, her cheeks flushed. "I just—"

"No, no." Ellen waved a hand. "Don't apologize. I invited you here, remember?" She crossed the room toward Kate and glanced at the photographs on top of the chest. Then she laughed. "Oh dear. I think I know what you found."

Kate's blush faded a little at Ellen's relaxed tone. Surely she'd read too much into the picture.

"The two of you looked very happy." It was the only thing she could think of to say. She tried to ignore the sharp pang of jealousy in her stomach. *Don't be ridiculous*, she scolded herself. *That photograph has to be almost forty years old*. But however long it had been, it was still difficult to see Paul looking overjoyed to have his arm around another woman.

"We were very young." Ellen stepped beside Kate and lifted the picture from the top of the chest. "When you're that age, you think you know everything." She was silent for a moment, then she turned to look at Kate. She was still smiling, but in her eyes Kate could see all the grief for what she had lost, for opportunities missed. "I never realized how easily happiness could slip away until I lost Trevor. Now, I guess I treasure my happy memories all the more."

"You should come over for dinner one evening. I know Paul would love to see you," Kate found herself saying before she could stop and consider her words. The invitation was instinctual, a reaction to the pain in the other woman's face. She was sure Ellen was right. Her relationship with Paul was a part of her history and nothing more.

"Really?"

"Of course." Kate realized that Ellen was probably very lonely. "We'll set something up soon."

"That would be nice." Ellen reached out and placed her hand on Kate's arm. "You're so generous. I'd heard that, of course." She paused and smiled. They both laughed. "There aren't many women I know who would invite their husband's former fiancée over for dinner."

Ellen set the picture down and turned back toward the painting, but Kate found herself rooted to the spot. *Fiancée?* Paul had never said anything about Ellen being his fiancée.

"You and Paul were actually engaged?"

Ellen laughed. "Well, as with a lot of things in the past, I guess the story depends on whom you ask."

Kate tried to smile but was only half successful. Ellen was right. The truth about the past often depended on a person's point of view, but Kate couldn't help the little flame of worry that sparked to life in her mind. She just wished Paul had given her a little more information about how close he and Ellen Harrington had been. Like any wife, she accepted that her husband had a past, but it came as a bit of a shock to see it immortalized on top of Ellen Carruthers' chest of drawers.

Between the two of them, Kate and Ellen managed to lift the large painting off the wall and carry it into the living room for closer inspection. Kate tried to concentrate on the task at hand, but Ellen's innocent comment had thrown her for a loop. Paul had never mentioned Ellen Harrington being anything other than his college sweetheart, but if Ellen said they were engaged, Paul would surely have known about it. And if he had known, why hadn't he shared that information with her?

"How did you know that this painting was one of the clues?" Kate asked, trying to distract herself from obsessing about Paul's apparent lack of candor. "Did your grandmother tell you?"

Ellen reached for the cord on the blinds that covered the windows. Outside, the sounds of students traveling to and from classes drifted on the refreshing early fall breeze. "Yes. In the letter she left me, she listed the paintings and said they would help me find my grandfather's second will. This painting was on the list."

"But I'm still confused about why she hid the will in the first place."

"She said she wanted to protect me. If Oliver had known there was another will, he would never have let it rest, even if I'd shown no interest in trying to claim my inheritance. The legal bills alone would have bankrupted my husband and me." She paused. "Oliver Coats is a very determined man. He would have made our lives miserable until I relinquished any claim to the Harrington property."

"But isn't he quite wealthy already?" Kate knew he owned a construction firm that did projects all across the southeast.

"It's not the money that matters to Oliver," Ellen said with a slight shudder. "It's the control and the power."

"And the other paintings that were on your grandmother's list?" Kate asked. "Do you have any idea who might have them?"

"I only know about one. And it belongs to Oliver. Well, to Carol, I guess, technically. But it's all the same thing."

"I see." Kate stared out the window for a moment, lost in thought. So far, the pieces of this puzzle weren't quite adding up. "So your grandmother hid the will to keep you out of the old family feud?"

"Yes. I moved away from here to escape all the unpleasantness. Her letter said she left me the clues so I could decide whether I wanted to get involved or not. If I wanted to let it go, well, then no one but me ever had to know there was a second will."

"Are you sure no one else knows about it? I can't imagine how hard it would be to keep a secret like that from the family."

"If anyone knows, they never said anything to me."

Kate looked at the painting again. "Have you checked under the frame, around the edges, that sort of thing? Perhaps there's a hidden message there."

Ellen nodded. "That was the first thing I thought of when I couldn't see anything obvious in the painting itself. But there's nothing. I took the frame off and gave it a thorough going over."

"May I see the list of paintings?"

Ellen reached for a piece of paper on the coffee table. "I've written down the information for you. It's a start at least."

Kate took the paper and read it over. Five paintings were listed by title, along with the size of the canvas. *High Hoot Ridge. The Beginning. Progress Comes to Harrington. Double Duty. Where My Heart Rests.*

"If only the titles of the last four were as clear as the first one," Kate said, "it would make looking for them a little easier." She rubbed her chin with one hand as she held the list with the other and read it over again. "Do you know which one of the paintings your cousin and her husband own?"

"No. Not a clue." Ellen paused. "But I still think Oliver's the best place to start, if you don't mind going to see him alone. I just don't think we'd get anywhere with him if I went."

"Are you sure you don't want to come?" Kate asked.

Ellen nodded. "Like I said, he'd never agree to see me. But he might agree to see you. He's always been very proud of his art collection, and he's been known to give private tours of his home."

Kate wasn't sure she liked the idea of getting in the middle of family feuds, not to mention approaching Oliver Coats on her own. Not after what Ellen had told her about him. "I doubt he'd just let me waltz in and poke around for the right painting."

"Well, I don't know about that. You have a certain way about you that makes people open up." Ellen reached over to squeeze Kate's arm.

Something in the other woman's touch filled Kate's heart with compassion. "Are you sure you want to get caught up in all of this? Maybe your grandmother was right, and you'd be better off staying out of it."

Ellen's cheeks flushed, and she lowered her head. "I wish I could," she said, lifting her eyes to meet Kate's. "But my late husband and I . . . well, we weren't always as frugal as we should have been." She sighed. "The truth is, Kate, I really need my share of money from the sale of the land. My husband's medical expenses were significant."

Suddenly Kate realized that Ellen wasn't living in the small faculty apartment for convenience. She was a widow with little money, and retirement fast approaching. No wonder she was concerned. In that case, Kate would just have to muster her courage and confront Oliver Coats in his den. Maybe he wouldn't turn out to be quite as ferocious as Ellen portrayed.

"All right, then. I'll find a way to talk with Oliver."

Ellen's face brightened. "Thank you."

"In the meantime, I'll see what I can do to track down these other paintings." Kate knew that her best friend Livvy Jenner, Copper Mill's head librarian, could be counted on to help with that part of the search. "Can you make me a list of who else might have an interest in the property? Or any other relative who could have inherited one of the paintings?"

"Of course . . . Although it won't be a long one."

Ellen grabbed a pen and wrote a few names on Kate's list of paintings.

"I'm afraid there aren't many members of the Harrington clan left," she said as she handed the information to Kate.

Kate glanced over the list. If Ellen Carruthers had little money, she had even less family.

"Most of them are second or third cousins that I haven't seen since childhood," Ellen added. "And I don't know any of the women's married names."

"It's a start," Kate reassured her. "We'll take this one step at a time."

"Would you like some more tea?" Ellen asked.

Kate looked at her watch. "No, thank you. I'd better be going. And I'll be in touch about Oliver. But first let me help you rehang that painting."

The two women carried the canvas back to its home above Ellen's bed. As Kate left the room, she couldn't help casting one last glance at the photograph on the chest of drawers. Her husband's smiling face was entirely familiar, yet at that moment, she had the sinking feeling she didn't know him quite as well as she thought she did.

Chapter Four

That evening, Kate pulled a chicken out of the oven and studied it with a critical eye. The crisp, brown bird gave off a heavenly aroma of lemon and rosemary. She sniffed it appreciatively and smiled.

Paul had suggested eating out that evening at the Bristol, an upscale restaurant inside the Hamilton Springs Hotel. But as much as Kate enjoyed dining out, she was ready for a night at home alone with her husband. Plus, it never hurt to remind him how much he enjoyed her cooking . . . especially when his former girlfriend had his picture displayed on her chest of drawers.

As if on cue, Kate heard the sound of Paul's pickup coming up the driveway. She quickly slid the dinner rolls into the oven, then began to stir the green beans on the stove as the garage door slammed.

"Katie? I'm home."

Even after almost thirty years of marriage, the sound of Paul's voice could still make her insides as mushy as the southern-style green beans she loved so much. Kate smoothed her hair, untied her apron, and brushed at some lint on her blue sweater. She'd never be mistaken for Betty Crocker or June Cleaver, but every once in a while, it didn't hurt for a husband to come home to a well-coiffed wife and a delicious, hot meal.

"I'm in the kitchen," she called as she headed for the living room to greet him.

"Wow." Paul stopped in his tracks a few feet away from her. "You look great! What's the occasion?"

Kate waved a hand in an airy motion. "I just thought it would be good for us to have a nice dinner together."

"Whew." Paul pretended to wipe sweat from his brow. "I was afraid maybe I'd forgotten some important anniversary."

Kate laughed. "Dinner will be ready in ten minutes," she said. "If you want to wash up . . ." She let her words trail off, hoping he would take the hint. His smile told her he was on to her.

"Okay, okay. I get it. It's one of those no-special-occasion special occasions."

Kate grinned. "Exactly."

Paul took her into his arms and gave her a kiss. "Beautiful wife, delicious dinner. If I didn't know any better, I'd say you were up to something."

Kate's heart thudded in her chest, but not from her husband's embrace. "Who, me?"

"Sure, act innocent," he teased.

"Go on now." Kate shooed him toward the bathroom before he could detect any signs of guilt. "We can eat as soon as the rolls are done."

He was back in a few minutes, wearing a fresh polo

shirt and khakis. His damp salt-and-pepper hair was neatly combed, and his vivid blue eyes sparkled. Looking like that, he brought to Kate's mind the much younger man who had courted her all those years ago.

"How's this?" Paul asked, presenting himself for her approval.

"Perfect," she replied. "Now have a seat, and I'll serve."

Kate had set out the good china—their wedding china to be exact.

Paul noticed the plate when he sat down at the kitchen table, and he traced the gold rim with one finger. "You're going all out tonight. Did you have this planned before or after I asked if you wanted to eat at the Bristol?" He winked at her. "You could give those folks a run for their money."

"I try," Kate replied in a lighthearted tone as she scurried around the tiny parsonage kitchen.

It didn't take long to set the food on the table and fill their iced tea glasses. Paul said grace over the meal, then he offered to carve the chicken. Kate handed him the knife and dished up the rest of the food.

"How was your day?" she asked, grateful for the reassuring familiarity of their dinner routine.

Kate and Paul had made a point of eating dinner together as a family almost every night when the kids were young, and even though Andrew, Melissa and Rebecca were now grown and gone, she and Paul had continued the tradition. Surprisingly, it was often harder to find time to eat dinner together now than when they had lived in San Antonio.

Who would have guessed that a small town like Copper Mill would keep them even more active and involved than they'd been in the big city? Kate was thankful, though, that her new home hadn't turned out to be a sleepy backwater town.

"Well, my first chamber of commerce meeting was an eye-opener, to say the least," Paul answered. He took a bite of chicken and made appreciative noises as he chewed. "Delicious, Kate."

"Thanks. So is your new position on the chamber going to take up a lot of your time?"

"Well, the coffee-and-pie routine might get a bit onerous, but I'll have to make the sacrifice." He grinned and gave her a wink. "Other than that, I'm not sure it will amount to much." His smile faded.

"Really? Why not?"

Kate had worried some when Paul had first told her about the mayor's invitation to join the chamber. Paul was already as busy as he'd been when he was the senior pastor of their large church in San Antonio. It was a different kind of busy, though. He spent more time with people than overseeing programs, and she could tell he was enjoying himself despite the long hours.

"As near as I can tell, the purpose of the Copper Mill Chamber of Commerce is to discourage outsiders from setting foot within the city limits."

Kate chuckled. "Are you sure you're not exaggerating a little?"

"Not much. There are only five members, including

me, and none of them seem inclined to do much to promote the city or develop the economic base. They're all too scared of being taken over by big-box retailers or corporations."

"Well, I can understand their fears. The dress shop in Pine Ridge that I thought was so cute just closed its doors. Someone told me it was because they couldn't compete with the discount stores."

"I know, but ignoring the problems in the community won't make them go away."

"Of course not," she agreed. "So, did they ask you to contribute anything?"

Paul paused, his fork halfway to his mouth. His cheeks turned pink. "Well, actually . . ."

Kate didn't like the sound of that. "What is it?"

"How would you feel about organizing the Christmas Craft Extravaganza?"

Kate chuckled, but when she looked at Paul again, she realized he wasn't kidding. "What have you volunteered me for?"

Paul held up both hands in self-defense. "I didn't volunteer you for anything. I just said I'd ask. And you don't have to do it if you don't want to. Honestly."

Kate sighed. "I'll think about it."

She had to admit she'd probably enjoy that kind of project. Several people had already suggested she get a booth at the annual event for her stained glass pieces, but the timing wasn't great. She had just started her art history class, not to mention taking on a new mystery.

"What other business did this august body of men conduct?" Kate asked.

Paul sighed. "Other than delegating the craft extravaganza? Well, let's see. There was some mention of a Men's Golf Scramble in October, but nobody wanted to be in charge of it. And meeting with Luke Danvers, the representative from the state's community development office, was roundly vetoed."

Kate put down her fork. "Wow."

"Yeah. Wow."

"So other than organizing social events and the odd ribbon cutting, what exactly does the Copper Mill Chamber of Commerce do?"

"I'm still trying to figure that out." He grimaced. "What's worse, I ran into Mike Rowland outside the bank. His job in Nashville didn't pan out, and now he's off to Chattanooga, hoping to get some construction work. Ever since we moved here, I've watched young people leave, one after another. I know it's not unusual, but still . . ."

Kate hated to see her husband so troubled, but as always, she admired his compassion. "I'm surprised that Lawton and the others aren't more concerned about the young people moving away."

"Oh, they're concerned all right. They just don't want to entertain any newfangled ideas, even though some changes might reverse the trend."

Kate looked at her husband thoughtfully. He often took on problems larger than any one man could handle, but he was also a proven leader with good ideas.

"Do you have some suggestions for the chamber as to what it should be doing?"

"I do. Remember when I was part of Leadership San Antonio?"

Kate nodded. Paul had made a substantial time commitment to participate in the networking and informational class for civic leaders. At the time, she'd hated to see him commit one more evening a week away from home, but in the end, it had been worth it. The class had opened doors for Paul to contribute to the community beyond the walls of the church.

"I think there are some basic things that the chamber could be doing. I even thought about calling my friend Bill Rohde from the tourism board in San Antonio to see what he thinks. But Lawton and the others are so resistant to change, it may not be possible to get them off square one."

Kate reached over to pat his hand. "If anyone can persuade them, it would be you."

"Thanks, Katie," he said, giving her hand a squeeze. Then he grimaced. "I wish I had as much faith in my persuasive abilities as you do. These Copper Mill nuts may be pretty tough to crack."

Kate laughed, then Paul did too when he realized how his last remark might be misconstrued.

"And on that note," Kate said, reaching for the empty plates to carry them to the sink, "how about some dessert?"

Paul winced. "After pie and coffee at the diner this afternoon, I'm afraid that might be pushing my luck."

"As long as you don't say Loretta's pies are better than mine, I think you'll be okay."

Paul laughed as Kate hoped he would.

"I may be adventurous, but I'm not *that* brave," he teased.

LATER, AFTER THEY had cleaned up the kitchen and were settled on the couch for the evening, Kate broached another topic.

"I was at Ellen Carruthers' place today after class."

"Who?" Paul looked up from the preaching journal he'd been perusing.

"Ellen Harrington Carruthers. Your former flame." Kate watched his face closely to measure his response.

"What did you talk about?"

Kate recounted that morning's conversation with Ellen, telling about her agreement to visit Oliver Coats.

"So I need a reason to visit the Coatses and ask to see one of the paintings they have in their possession."

Paul's eyes were lined with worry. "He's not dangerous, is he?"

"I don't think so. Just unpleasant."

"And Ellen didn't have any suggestions about how to approach him?"

"No, the only thing she could come up with was posing as an art collector . . ." Kate's voice was filled with doubt.

"And you don't like that idea."

"No. I don't want to be duplicitous. I'd like to have a legitimate reason for contacting the Coatses."

Paul was quiet for a long moment, and then his eyes lit up.

"Tell me about your class. Do you have a big paper or a project for the semester?"

Kate nodded. "We have to do a presentation on an American artist of our—" She stopped and then she smiled. "Paul Hanlon, have I told you lately that you're brilliant?"

His eyes twinkled. "Now that you mention it, no. I don't think there's been much commenting on my genius around here in recent days."

Kate clapped her hands together. "This is perfect. I can kill two birds with one stone."

"Just be careful who's in your line of fire when you start slinging those stones," Paul advised her. "You're not being dishonest with Oliver and Carol Coats, but you're not being completely truthful either."

"I'll watch my step," Kate said. "Don't worry."

He reached over and stroked her hair. "I'm pretty sure I'll worry anyway." Paul gave her a lopsided grin. "It's inevitable when your wife is the Copper Mill equivalent of Miss Marple."

Kate laughed, then added as casually as she could, "By the way, I mentioned to Ellen that we'd like to have her over for dinner one evening."

"It would be good to see her again. She was always a good conversationalist. But I understand if it's not the most comfortable thing in the world for you to invite my ex over for dinner."

"It's been a while since you've seen her, huh?" Kate

said, hoping to draw a more informative response out of him.

Paul looked thoughtful for a moment, and then a rueful smile played around the corners of his mouth. "Since she moved to the northeast for graduate school, I guess. That was a long time ago."

"It's a shame the two of you lost touch." Kate wished she could stop herself from digging for information, but that photo in Ellen's bedroom had been troubling her.

Paul shrugged. "Back then phone calls were expensive. And I was never much of a letter writer."

"She said her mom talked to yours and kept her up to date on what you were doing."

"*Hmm.* That's nice." Paul picked up the journal and began leafing through the pages.

Kate sighed. Clearly the subtle approach wasn't going to work when it came to eliciting the information she wanted.

"So I know you two were pretty serious . . ."

He paused, closed the journal, and laid it on his lap. "Yeah, well, we were together for a few years. What makes you so curious about Ellen's and my relationship?"

Kate didn't think Paul was being deliberately obtuse, but then, sometimes that was the difference between women and men. One of her old boyfriends could turn up for dinner, and she doubted that Paul would bat an eyelash.

"Well, it's not every day that a wife ends up with her husband's old flame for a professor," she teased.

Paul chuckled. "That was well over thirty years ago, Kate."

"Ellen still has a picture of the two of you on display with her family photos." The words came out before she could stop them.

This seemed to get at least a minimal response from Paul. "A photo? Huh. Well, what do you know."

Kate didn't know whether to pull her hair out or be relieved. Clearly Paul considered Ellen nothing more than an old girlfriend. If they'd ever been engaged, he would surely have mentioned it. Perhaps Ellen had been mistaken. As Paul had pointed out, they had dated well over thirty years ago. Memories could fade, and people sometimes made more of events than the facts warranted. She told herself that she shouldn't waste another moment's thought on it.

"Anything good on television tonight?" Paul asked, changing the subject.

Kate was happy to let it go, because *she* was the one curled up on the couch next to Paul. A fact for which she would be forever grateful.

Chapter Five

The next morning, Kate rose early, as was her custom, and settled into her favorite rocking chair for a few quiet moments before another busy day commenced. She was apprehensive about calling Oliver and Carol Coats to schedule the meeting, and she had long ago found that when she was worried, she was much better off turning to God for help rather than trying to go it alone.

She opened her well-worn Bible and turned to a familiar passage—the parables of "lost things," as Paul called them. First was the shepherd who went looking for the one sheep out of a hundred that had wandered away. Then came the woman who searched tirelessly for her lost silver coin until she found it. Finally, of course, was the most familiar parable of all: the story of the lost son.

Kate paused to read the familiar words once more. They gave her a little more insight into how Ellen Carruthers must have felt coming home and not expecting any welcome from her family. Although Ellen clearly hadn't lived a prodigal's life, Kate realized that, like the prodigal son, Ellen must still have had a strong need to belong. Perhaps that was why she kept the picture of Paul—more as an anchor to the past than a memorial to an old love. Kate hoped that was the case. She liked Ellen, but she also knew that lonely people were vulnerable. They sometimes tried to recreate what they'd lost.

Oliver Coats, on the other hand, sounded much like the resentful older brother in the parable. If Oliver refused to even speak to Ellen, Kate was sure he wasn't about to kill the fatted calf for the homecoming of his wife's long-absent cousin.

The long-standing dispute had evidently begun with Carol and Ellen's great-grandfathers and continued to the present. Even if Kate solved the mystery, she knew it wouldn't solve the problem of Ellen's loneliness. The money from the sale of the land would help Ellen financially, but a reconciliation between her and her cousin Carol would be far more valuable. And in the long run, it might be the most rewarding result of Kate's efforts to track down the paintings and find the missing will.

"Lord, put me on the right path," Kate prayed softly. "And help me to be as faithful as the shepherd, as diligent as the woman in her search for that coin, and as loving as the father who welcomed home his lost son."

Kate closed her Bible and held it in her lap for a moment, drinking in the stillness of the morning. For all the satisfaction she had experienced in solving mysteries in Copper Mill, she found helping people rebuild their relationships even more rewarding.

With that thought in mind, she stood up and walked to the telephone to call Oliver Coats.

SEVERAL DAYS LATER on a sunny Monday morning, Kate stood on the sidewalk in front of Oliver and Carol Coats' enormous Victorian home in Pine Ridge. Beneath the shade of towering elms, the house dominated the quiet residential street. Gables, gingerbread trim, balconies, and a wraparound front porch made the home resemble Scarlett O'Hara's bonnet.

Kate took a deep breath and headed up the walk.

Ellen's cousin Carol and her husband were expecting Kate Hanlon, art student, not Kate Hanlon, sleuth. She felt a twinge of guilt, but given Oliver Coats' treatment of Ellen, Kate limited herself to a twinge. Besides, thanks to Paul, she wasn't lying about her reason for wanting to speak with Oliver. Her art history project was a legitimate excuse.

Kate's low-heeled pumps tapped against the porch steps as she made her way toward the door. With no doorbell in evidence, she knocked on the screen door. For several long moments, the house remained silent, and Kate wondered whether the Coatses had forgotten the appointment. But then she heard footsteps inside, and a moment later, the door opened to reveal a middle-aged brunette in an old-fashioned print dress. The woman looked like June Cleaver's dark-haired twin.

"Hello—" Kate began.

"Kate Hanlon?" the woman asked. Her furrowed brow indicated perpetual worry.

"That's me." Kate smiled, hoping to alleviate the other woman's concern.

The woman unlatched the screen door and opened it. "Come in. I'm Carol Coats."

"Thank you." Kate sensed that her presence somehow distressed the woman. "I hope I'm not early," she added, even though she knew she was exactly on time.

"No, no. You're fine." But Carol's fluttering hands gave away her discomfort.

"Your husband is expecting me," Kate offered, unsure what else to say to the nervous woman, who was now practically wringing her hands.

"He is." Carol cast a quick glance over her shoulder and then turned back to Kate. "Would you follow me?"

"Of course." Kate forced a smile, trying to ignore the other woman's strange behavior.

Ellen's cousin seemed more like a servant than the lady of the house. And her anxiety was contagious. Kate's heart was beating faster than usual.

Carol led Kate through the foyer and into a long corridor. Kate darted quick glances into each room as they passed. Beautiful antiques vied with luxurious oriental rugs for prominence beneath the nine-foot ceilings. Intricate molding and gleaming hardwood floors completed the lavish picture. The home had been painstakingly restored. Clearly the sale of the disputed land wasn't a financial necessity for this branch of the Harrington clan.

At the rear of the home, Kate's hostess turned to the right, and Kate found herself entering an exquisite sun porch decorated in peach and cream. The dark wicker furniture boasted thick cushions, and here again several antiques—a beautiful inlaid occasional table and a small sideboard—added a restrained elegance to the room.

"Please have a seat. Oliver will be with you in a moment." And then to Kate's consternation, Carol Coats disappeared far more quickly than she'd answered the door. Kate was left alone, when what she'd really wanted was the chance to learn more about Ellen's cousin. She sat down on the wicker sofa and placed her handbag in her lap. In the quiet, she could hear a clock ticking from another room. The sun porch was warm, the air a bit stuffy. Several minutes passed, and Kate had begun to wonder whether Oliver would come, when a tall masculine figure appeared in the doorway.

"Kate?" With his height and reserved manner, Oliver Coats was certainly intimidating.

Kate rose to her feet. "Yes. And you must be Oliver."

He smiled, and the effect changed his appearance entirely so that he looked almost handsome.

"Please, sit down," he said, moving toward the chair opposite her. "I understand you're interested in some pieces in my collection?"

Kate forced a smile. "Yes. I'm doing a class project on your wife's great-aunt, Lela Harrington. I thought it would be interesting to focus on a local artist."

Oliver looked puzzled. "For a class project, you say?"

Kate nodded. "I'm an artist myself, in stained glass. I'm taking a class at Pine Ridge College for . . . well, for inspiration, I guess."

"How did you learn about my wife's great-aunt?"

His dark eyes pierced through her, and Kate swallowed. She knew she would have to navigate a fine line.

"My professor showed me an example of her work. Her style is very striking. My professor said that Mrs. Harrington was known as the Grandma Moses of Pine Ridge."

Oliver didn't reply, but he looked thoughtful.

"My professor suggested that if I was interested in learning more about her grandmother's work, I should contact you. She thought you might have some artwork of hers that I could use for my project." Kate wondered if Oliver would mention his estrangement from his wife's cousin. "If you do, I was hoping that you might let me photograph—"

Oliver frowned. "I don't think—"

"I can photograph without a flash if you're worried about the artwork deteriorating."

"Actually, I only have one of Lela Harrington's paintings." He shifted in his seat and ran a finger around the inside of his collar. "I have to apologize . . ." He paused and smiled again as if to turn on the charm. "I hadn't realized just how warm it is in here. Would you like a glass of iced tea?"

"That would be lovely." Anything to prolong her visit. She'd learned in her sleuthing that the longer she could keep people talking, the more likely they were to reveal important information.

"Carol!" Oliver practically shouted.

Kate jumped and then tried to pretend she hadn't been startled. Oliver's mousy wife appeared in the doorway almost immediately.

"Iced tea, please." He was curt with his wife, but when he turned back to Kate, his expression was as pleasant as could be. "Do you prefer sweetened or unsweetened?"

"Whatever you have," Kate said, hoping to ease the burden on Carol.

"We have both," Oliver said decisively, and Kate felt a pang of sympathy for his wife. Oliver was clearly something of a despot in his own home. "Carol, just bring a tray with both kinds of tea."

Carol nodded and disappeared again.

"Now," Oliver said, "if you'll come with me, I can show you the painting."

Kate followed obediently—did anyone follow Oliver Coats any other way?—as he retraced her earlier route through the house. Halfway down the long corridor, he turned into one of the rooms.

"Here it is." Oliver walked to the middle of the room, then gestured to a spot over the fireplace.

Kate recognized Lela Harrington's work at once. This painting, though, was nothing like the one Ellen owned. Hers was a gentle scene of High Hoot Ridge. Oliver's painting portrayed the ironworks in full operation, with heavy streams of black smoke rising from the blast furnace and streaming across the canvas. Even the apple trees at the edge of the clearing looked wan and sickly. Where High Hoot Ridge had once been peaceful and pastoral, this work showed the ruinous effects of industrialization on the beautiful scenery.

"It's very dramatic, isn't it?" Kate stepped closer to

study the painting. "Even in the Primitive style, you can feel the impact of people on the environment."

Kate looked over her shoulder in time to catch Oliver rolling his eyes. He quickly stopped when he realized Kate was watching him.

"I doubt Lela Harrington meant this painting as a commentary on anything. More likely, she was painting a scene from memory."

"She was alive while the ironworks were still in operation?"

"Just at the end. She would have been a very small child."

"Yet it must have made quite an impression on her."

Oliver moved to stand beside her, his gaze on the painting. "How much do you know about the ironworks?"

Kate hesitated. She wouldn't be untruthful, but she also didn't have to reveal everything she knew.

At that moment, Kate saw movement out of the corner of her eye. Carol entered the room carrying a tray with two pitchers of iced tea and two tall glasses.

"I'm sorry to take so long," she said, more to Oliver than to Kate. She set the tray on a sideboard just inside the door.

"Oh, what lovely crystal," Kate said before Oliver could speak. "Is it antique?"

She continued to make small talk while Carol poured the tea and handed glasses to Kate and Oliver. Oliver gestured for Carol to sit in a chair in the corner of the room.

"So," Kate said several minutes later in an effort to

bring the conversation back to the painting, "what happened to the ironworks? Why was it abandoned?"

Oliver grimaced. "A family feud, unfortunately. The ironworks was profitable, but for years the ore had to be brought down from the ridge by mule cart. In the late 1800s, other ironworks began building railroad spurs up to their works so they could move the ore faster. Carol's great-grandfather and his brother disagreed about building a spur to High Hoot Ridge. The brother was against it, and Carol's great-grandfather couldn't build without his brother's consent." Oliver's voice was bitter, as if he'd personally participated in the disagreement between the brothers.

"And that shut down the ironworks?" Kate asked.

"Not immediately." Oliver took a long drink of his iced tea. "But eventually the brothers couldn't keep up with their competition. By the time they died, they'd closed up the ironworks, and Harrington, the company town, was abandoned. The only remaining legacy was the name of the county."

"Were there ever any attempts to reopen the ironworks?"

"Carol's grandfather considered it, but by then . . . well, it wasn't worth the investment that would have been necessary to make them operational again."

"So it's all still there, on High Hoot Ridge?"

Oliver nodded. "For now. Although I expect it to be sold shortly."

"Sold?" Kate tried to hide her surprise. Ellen had mentioned the offer from the state, but the sale hadn't sounded imminent. "To whom?"

"A paper company," Oliver answered. "They can make good use of the land."

Kate bit her lip to hide her surprise at this news. She wanted to ask more questions, but she didn't want to draw Oliver's suspicions, so she changed the subject.

"Have you ever been up there?" Kate asked, looking at Carol.

"Not since she was a child," Oliver said, answering for his wife. "No need, really. What's there to see?"

Kate wondered that anyone could be so indifferent to his wife's heritage. "Yet you put the painting in a place of prominence?"

Oliver shrugged. "It's a valuable piece of art. And it does hold some sentimental value, I suppose."

Kate could understand why Ellen wasn't fond of her cousin's husband. His arrogance and coldhearted pragmatism weren't very endearing.

"May I photograph it then?" she asked.

"Only for personal use," Oliver said in a warning tone. "I don't want to come across the image on the Internet or on some cheap reproduction . . ."

"Just for my class project," she assured him.

She pulled her digital camera from her handbag. As she adjusted the settings and turned off the flash to avoid damaging the painting, she continued her efforts to draw information from Oliver while Carol sat in the corner, her eyes focused on the floor.

Kate framed the painting in her viewfinder and bit her tongue. She could feel Oliver's eyes boring into the back of her head. Clearly he felt Kate was tainted by her association with Ellen.

"Has anyone else expressed interest in buying the land?" Kate couldn't resist asking the question, though she knew she was playing with fire.

Oliver sniffed, whether in triumph or disdain Kate wasn't sure.

"The state expressed an interest in turning the area into a wildlife preserve, but their offer was far less than the commercial one."

Kate remembered Ellen's lyrical description of High Hoot Ridge, the way she'd brought the town to life with her words, the treasured time she'd spent with her grandmother at the ironworks. Clearly Oliver felt no emotional connection to the property.

"You won't be sorry to let go of the land?" she asked Carol. "You must have spent time there as a child."

Kate finished taking pictures, turned off the camera, and stowed it back in her handbag. She looked expectantly at Carol, but the woman continued staring at the floor.

Oliver drained the last of his iced tea and set the glass down on the sideboard with a *thunk*. Kate winced at the danger to the valuable crystal.

"The past has never held much appeal for Carol," Oliver said. "The future is what matters. And once the deal goes through, we can put this old family dispute behind us once and for all."

Of course he wanted to see the sale go through quickly, Kate thought. She wondered whether it was merely his greed that made him so eager or if he had any idea about the missing will that might interfere with his plans.

"When do you expect the sale to be final?" Kate asked.

A shadow crossed Oliver's face, and she realized she'd pushed the conversation too far.

"I thought you were interested in the artwork," he said, his eyes darkening with suspicion. "Not an old family squabble."

"I'm sorry. I didn't mean to sound nosy. The history behind the painting could be important to my project. Knowing what motivated the artist to paint certain scenes or people, that sort of thing."

"From what I've been told, Lela Harrington was forever tromping around the ridge with her easel and her paints. You won't find many canvases of hers that aren't somehow connected to the town or the ironworks." He glanced at his watch. "I don't mean to be rude, but I have an appointment in twenty minutes."

"Of course. I'm sorry." Kate gave him an apologetic smile. "I didn't mean to monopolize your time."

"I'm always happy to share pieces from my collection," Oliver said, and she could see he meant the words. Not from a sense of generosity, Kate was sure, but because of the prestige it added to his position in Pine Ridge's social hierarchy.

"This will help so much with my project," Kate said. She turned to the silent Carol. "And thank you for the iced tea."

"Carol will see you out," Oliver said.

They exchanged good-byes, and Kate gratefully followed her hostess to the front door.

"It was nice to meet you," she said as she stepped outside.

Carol smiled sadly.

"You too. We don't get a lot of visitors." She blushed, then gave a little wave as she closed the front door.

Kate was left alone on the porch. What a strange couple. And there'd certainly been nothing in Oliver Coats' behavior to contradict anything Ellen had told her. He was conceited and condescending, but at least she now had a picture of the painting for her second clue. She'd head home and print out her photographs. Then she'd set up a time to meet with Ellen.

Kate hadn't seen any obvious indication in the painting of where the will might be hidden. A big red X, for example, would have been helpful. But the clues must be there somewhere if Ellen's grandmother had meant for her to find them.

Kate walked to her car, unlocked the door, and slid inside. She'd had no idea what she would be getting herself into by signing up for a course at Pine Ridge College. Her class project might very well turn out to be more difficult than anything she might have dreamed up on her own.

Chapter Six

After class the next day, Kate waited patiently while the other students filed out of the room. Two or three of them approached Professor Carruthers to speak with her about their projects, so it was much later by the time Ellen turned her attention to Kate.

"Well?" Ellen was as eager as Kate to discuss Kate's meeting with Oliver Coats. "How did it go?" she asked as they settled into a couple of chairs near the front of the classroom.

"You were right about Oliver." Kate grimaced. "He certainly thinks well of himself."

"Did he show you the painting?" Ellen came straight to the point. The dark circles under her eyes testified to the strain she'd been under in recent days.

"Yes." Kate was glad to have some good news for her. "He was surprisingly accommodating. Even had Carol fix iced tea. She seemed to walk on eggshells around him though."

"Poor Carol." Ellen pushed a lock of hair off her face. "She always was shy and retiring. I can't imagine what all these years with Oliver have done to her."

"I think the strongest person would show signs of wear and tear, if they were always on the receiving end of such overbearing behavior." Kate reached into her handbag. "But he did allow me to take photographs of the painting."

She spread out the glossy prints she'd printed from her computer on top of the desk. "Do you recognize it?"

Ellen picked up the photo on top of the pile and traced a finger over the image, as if reliving a well-loved memory.

"The ironworks," she said, her voice wistful. "Carol and I played there often as children." She made a sound that was half laugh, half sigh. "Some of our other cousins played there with us. Our mothers didn't like it. They thought it far too dangerous. But we promised never to go near the blast furnace, so they let us go."

"And did you?" Kate asked, intrigued by this glimpse into Ellen's past. "Go near the old blast furnace, I mean."

Ellen chuckled. "Of course we did. It made the best tunnel for playing bandits, and when you stood in the middle and looked up the chimney, you could see right up to the sky." She paused. "I'd love to see the painting itself."

Kate picked up one of the photos. "I took each section of the painting and enlarged the photo. I didn't see anything obvious that looks like a clue." The almost childlike style of the paintings would have made it difficult to conceal anything significant.

"*Hmm*." Ellen took a long time to study each enlargement. "I don't see anything here either. I suppose the clue could have been hidden under the frame or on the edges of the canvas, but Oliver would never agree to having the frame examined. Though I think we'd have found something on my painting if that were the case."

Kate nodded in agreement. "So, we have your landscape and now the painting of the ironworks. Both are of the same location. Perhaps that's the clue?"

Ellen shrugged. "There's no way to know unless we can get our hands on the other three paintings. Did Oliver give any indication of where they might be?"

Kate shook her head. "So what should we do next?" Ellen asked.

"We'll have to start contacting the relatives you listed for me and see what they know."

Ellen grimaced. "That may prove more difficult than it sounds."

"I think my friend Livvy can help us out. She's an excellent researcher."

Ellen's face brightened. "So you think we really might be able to find all the paintings?"

"We can certainly try." Kate felt a pang of worry at the thought of just how time consuming this search might turn out to be.

Ellen leafed through the photos once again, her eyes wistful. "It's been a long time since I've thought about those times on High Hoot Ridge. I'd like to see it again someday."

"Why wait for someday? Why don't we go see it sometime next week?" Kate wanted to visit the place herself. If she was going to solve this mystery, every piece of information she could gather would help, including a sense of the place in question.

Ellen frowned. "But I have no claim to the property. We'd be trespassing."

"We can't do that, of course." Kate frowned, but then an idea occurred to her. "What if I contact Oliver for permission to visit the site? Pictures of the actual location could be a nice addition to my project."

When Kate presented her project, she wanted to have something to show besides the paintings themselves. The more she learned about the old town of Harrington, the more she wanted to know. So much history had been lost in the mists of time. Perhaps a small part of it could be salvaged.

Ellen gathered up the photos and handed them back to Kate. They rose from their chairs and made their way toward the door.

"Let me know what Oliver says." Ellen paused outside the room. "If he gives his permission, we can take a picnic lunch and make a day of it."

"I'll bring the food," Kate said.

The two women parted ways at the end of the corridor, Ellen heading for her office and Kate exiting the building toward her car.

As she drove home, Kate prayed for patience. She hadn't planned on any further dealings with the obnoxious

Oliver Coats, but there was no way around it. If she wanted to visit High Hoot Ridge and the abandoned town of Harrington, she was going to have to beard the lion in his den once more.

AS IT TURNED OUT, Kate found that securing Oliver's permission was quite simple. She left a message on his answering machine, and he left a response on hers. She chuckled as she listened to the rather lengthy rambling that not only elevated his own importance but condescended sufficiently to allow her to visit the property. His officiousness made Kate feel as if she needed a shower, but she was delighted to get the go-ahead for her visit. Since Ellen didn't teach any classes on Thursday, they decided on that day.

KATE ROSE AT five thirty on Thursday morning and padded to the kitchen to turn on the coffeemaker. When she'd poured herself a steaming cup of her favorite brew, she went to the living room and settled into her rocker. She spent some time in prayer, then she opened her Bible and turned to that day's reading. She smiled to herself when she saw the passage.

"I lift up my eyes to the hills—where does my help come from," she read out loud. "My help comes from the Lord, the Maker of heaven and earth." She'd always loved that selection from the Psalms, and it seemed particularly appropriate for their pilgrimage to High Hoot Ridge.

Later, after she kissed Paul good-bye and sent him off to work, she packed the picnic lunch for her day with

Ellen. She'd made her favorite chicken salad recipe that she always served tucked inside croissants. Fruit salad and sand tarts completed the meal. Kate packed the food in a wicker picnic basket and headed out the door.

Ellen was waiting on the curb outside her apartment at the college when Kate arrived. She wore an emerald green sweater and dark slacks. As Kate pulled up to the curb, she lifted a hand in greeting.

"Thank you for driving," Ellen said after she slid into the car and they exchanged a cheery hello. "It will be nice to look around rather than having to concentrate on the road." She clipped her seat belt around her waist and adjusted the shoulder strap. "I rarely ever drove when Trevor and I lived in New York."

"Well, I'm a Texas girl at heart," Kate replied with a grin. "I love to drive. Although the winding roads around here aren't conducive to my lead-footed tendencies."

Ellen laughed, then pulled a piece of paper from her handbag. "I printed a map off the Internet in case my memory fails me."

They drove east out of Pine Ridge and followed a winding two-lane highway toward the rolling mountains in the distance. The first hint of fall could be seen in the occasional specks of orange and yellow among the trees. In a few weeks, the foliage would be a symphony of reds, browns, and golds, but for now the landscape rested on the cusp of the changing seasons.

Kate drove carefully along the twisting road as it wound between two steep ridges. Fortunately, the hardwood forests of oak and hickory through this area had not yet been ravaged by the paper industry Oliver Coats was so eager to do business with. Of course, some companies followed the new, more ecologically sensitive practices that had been developed to preserve the environment. Kate wondered if the future owners of High Hoot Ridge fell into that category. She hoped so. The patchwork of greens contrasted with the jutting brown ridges reminded her that the hands of God had created this beauty, not human hands.

Beside Kate, Ellen seemed enthralled with the passing scenery. They drove for another fifteen minutes in silence before she spoke.

"I'd forgotten," she said in a quiet voice. "It's breathtaking, isn't it?"

Kate knew that the farther east they drove from Copper Mill and Pine Ridge, the more dramatic the scenery would become. But knowing something and seeing it with her own eyes were two very different things.

"Yes, breathtaking," she agreed.

"I think the turn is coming up," Ellen said after checking the map. "Look for a gas station and a dirt road just beyond it."

Sure enough, a few minutes later, they spotted the station, but it was far from what Kate had imagined it would look like. The roof of the abandoned building had collapsed, and weeds had grown up through the cracks in the cement paving. Two rusty, old-fashioned gas pumps leaned drunkenly toward each other as if they were whispering secrets.

"I don't think anyone's filled up their gas tank there in quite a while," Kate said as she slowed to make the turn.

Ellen's eyes were glued to the ramshackle building. "My grandparents used to stop there. And my grandfather would buy us Chocolate Soldiers and MoonPies."

Kate was familiar with MoonPies, those gooey Southern treats made with graham crackers and marshmallow fluff, but she'd never heard of the other treat.

"What's a Chocolate Soldier?"

"It was a bottled drink, not like chocolate milk exactly but similar. All the flavoring was at the bottom of the bottle, so you had to shake it up before you opened it to mix it up well."

"Sounds delicious. I've never met a form of chocolate I didn't like."

Ellen nodded. "Same with me. I'm a hopeless chocoholic."

They laughed, and Ellen continued to reminisce as the dirt road wound up the side of the ridge, leading to hairpin curves at each end. Kate gripped the steering wheel as she maneuvered the tighter curves beneath a canopy of trees. Whoever had named High Hoot Ridge hadn't been joking about the high part. Ellen must have noticed Kate's death grip on the wheel as they climbed.

"Sorry, Kate. I forgot to warn you about this road. It's one of the things that led to the demise of the ironworks."

"Oliver mentioned it," Kate replied. "He said your great-grandfather wouldn't agree to build a rail line to High Hoot Ridge."

"The Harringtons have always been known for their stubbornness. In the end, neither brother got what he wanted."

"Too bad there was no one to play King Solomon and resolve the dispute."

"Yes, it is. Instead, they lost almost all of their fortunes, and the people of Harrington lost everything."

"Where did those folks go?"

"I have no idea. By the time I came along, the abandoned ironworks and the town were nothing more than a playground for me and my cousins."

"Did someone still live up here then?"

"My grandmother did during the summer, if you can believe it. Our branch of the family built our home here in Harrington, while Carol's side built in Pine Ridge. The house you visited, in fact. But my grandmother stayed up here every summer until we had to move her to a nursing home."

Kate couldn't imagine living alone on the ridge, even for a few months out of the year.

They rounded one last curve, and finally Kate saw what they'd been looking for.

"There's Harrington," Ellen said, pointing toward the collection of abandoned buildings that made the gas station look like a palace.

"Oh." Kate wasn't sure what she'd been expecting, but somehow she'd formed a more romantic image of Harrington than this. Most of the buildings were little more than piles of weather-beaten lumber lost in a sea of weeds. Kudzu, that great equalizer in the South, twined through the remains as if trying to reclaim the abandoned town for Mother Nature.

"It does look bad, doesn't it?" Ellen sighed. Her eagerness had dimmed.

Kate pulled the car to a stop by the edge of the road. Ahead, she could still make out the faint track that had once been the bustling main street of Harrington.

"C'mon," Ellen said, "I'll show you around."

Kate stepped gingerly from the car, glad she'd worn sensible shoes. Rocks and pinecones littered the ground among the tall grass. She hoped there weren't any snakes. Kate loved the outdoors, but she wasn't fond of anything that slithered on its belly.

"This was the main street?" she asked as they picked their way between the decaying buildings.

"The only street," Ellen said. "On that side was the post office, the company store, and the livery," she said, gesturing toward the rubble. Then she turned and pointed toward the other side. "That building was the barber shop, and there, at the end, the hotel. And back in those woods was a dormitory for the single men."

While all the other buildings had been small one-story affairs, the town hotel looked as if it had consisted of at least two floors, maybe three.

"A little farther on was the church, which doubled as the schoolhouse. An itinerant Methodist preacher came through every so often to hold services. At least that's what my grandmother told me."

The combination church and schoolhouse had fared the best of any of the buildings in the little town. Its basic structure and steeple remained intact.

"Look," Kate said, raising her hand to shield her eyes from the sun. "Is that the church bell? Could it have survived all these years?"

They made their way closer to discover that, sure enough, the old bell still hung in the belfry below the steeple.

"I guess it was too much trouble to take down. Or maybe too heavy to move." Ellen looked at it thoughtfully. "I wonder if it still works."

Before Kate could say anything, Ellen clambered up the three short steps and ducked through the doorway into the old building.

"Wait!" Kate called, but it was too late.

She prayed the aging structure wouldn't crumple with Ellen trapped inside. A moment later, she heard the clear, rich pealing of the bell. The sound rang out over the ridge, echoing through the treetops. How many times had it summoned worshippers to Sunday services or children to their lessons? Had they rung it to summon help in times of distress? Hearing the sound, Kate could almost picture the little main street at the turn of the century, bustling with dozens of the former residents of Harrington. Strange to think that a good number of people had lived full and often difficult lives in this now-abandoned place.

Kate was so caught up visualizing the scene that she almost didn't hear the snapping of wood and the small cry that came from the abandoned church.

Chapter Seven

Ellen?" Kate moved toward the steps, concern in her voice. Most likely it had just been the building settling or some small animal scrabbling around inside. Kate mounted the steps until she reached the top and could peer into the gloomy interior.

"Ellen?" she called again, but there was no answer. The hairs on the back of Kate's neck stood up. She took a tentative step into the dark building, worried now that the sound she'd heard might have been a floorboard giving way beneath Ellen's weight.

If only she had a flashlight. She paused another moment for her eyes to adjust to the dimness. "Ellen, are you okay?" Her pulse fluttered in her throat. They were so isolated up here on the ridge. What if Ellen was hurt? How would she—

"Kate!"

Kate's heart swelled with relief at the sound of Ellen's voice. "I'm here. Keep talking, and I'll follow your voice."

"Okay. But hurry, please. I need your help."

Kate picked her way cautiously across what must have once been the church foyer.

"I'm coming," she reassured Ellen. She feared that the floor might collapse beneath her at any moment, but she kept going. Just past the foyer, she entered the larger room that had served as both classroom and sanctuary.

"Over here," Ellen called. "Can you see me?"

Kate followed the sound of her voice and spied her seated on a low platform at the front of the room that must have once held both the pulpit and the teacher's desk.

"I'm stuck," Ellen said. The panic receded from her voice at Kate's arrival.

Kate hustled across the room. "What happened?"

"I must have stepped on a rotten board. I think I'm okay, but my ankle's stuck." She gestured toward her right leg. Her foot had disappeared through the hole in the floorboard. "Can you help me get it out?"

"Let me see if I can find something to use as a crowbar," she said.

A few minutes' search finally turned up a long piece of metal that had probably been a brace of some kind. Kate used it to pry up the boards around Ellen's foot.

"Okay, pull," Kate instructed as she put all her weight on the end of the bar.

The floorboards squeaked in protest, but Ellen worked her foot free of the hole.

"It's out," she said, scooting to the side and rubbing her ankle. She gave a shaky laugh. "I can't believe that happened."

With that crisis averted, Kate could breathe again.

"Thank goodness it wasn't worse," she said, collapsing on the platform beside Ellen. "Does it hurt?"

Ellen flexed her foot. "No. I think it's okay. I'm just glad I didn't come up here alone. I don't think anyone would have ever found me."

"It's definitely not a place to get stuck," Kate agreed. "I can't believe your grandmother lived up here alone all those summers."

"Well, she probably had enough sense not to go tramping around in dilapidated buildings," Ellen said with a weak smile. "Let's get out of here, shall we?"

Kate rose and helped Ellen to her feet. "Can you walk?"

"Yes. No harm done, other than to my adrenal glands. I think they've gotten their workout for the year."

"Mine too," Kate agreed.

Together, they carefully picked their way back across the room to the outside door. Once they reached the steps, Kate breathed a sigh of relief. "Well, that's about enough excitement for one day, I think. Should we head home?"

To her surprise, Ellen shook her head. "I'm fine, really. More scared than hurt. And as long as we're here, I'd like to look around." She grinned. "I'll try to stay out of harm's way for the rest of the day."

"Do you want to head on up to the ironworks?" Kate asked. If Ellen wanted to keep going, Kate was game.

"Sure," Ellen said.

They returned to the main road and followed it up the ridge. A few hundred yards ahead, they stumbled into a clearing that contained the blast furnace and the remains of some other outlying buildings.

The air had become eerily still. Kate stepped forward as if she were as worried about dislodging ghosts as she was of encountering wayward reptiles.

"It's amazing." Kate couldn't think of any other word as her gaze took in the height of the blast furnace. It was almost as tall as the trees that surrounded the clearing.

Piles of slack rimmed the area, the natural result of smelting the ore. Strangely enough, the abandoned ironworks had an almost holy feel about it, as if it were home only to its creator and the few wild animals that lived in its shadow. Kate could understand how Lela Harrington had been able to paint it in its original state, before the coming of man, even though she'd never actually seen it that way.

Ellen walked ahead of Kate, pausing here and there to look more closely at the remains of the surrounding structures. "Those were the kilns," Ellen said, pointing to two brick structures that had started to cave in. "And the puddling furnace was there." She indicated the remains of a tall chimney that looked as if it was teetering on the edge of collapse.

"I wondered what those other buildings were in the second painting," Kate said. She hadn't realized how complicated it must have been to mine the iron ore and refine it.

"There's a grist mill and a saw mill too . . . over that way." Ellen nodded toward the ridge beyond the clearing. "Not quite enough room here for everything."

"I can see now why they needed a town," Kate said. "It must have taken a lot of employees to keep the works running."

"Most came from around the ridge. They lived in the hollows and climbed up here to work every morning."

Kate marveled at the hardiness of the folks who had made the ironworks hum on a daily basis. Theirs had not been an easy life.

"It's a shame people don't get a chance to see this," she said. "So much history."

Ellen nodded. "I often imagine it as it must have been back then, bustling with people and horses and with the smell of the furnaces on the breeze."

Kate looked around the clearing, her expression troubled. She hated to add to Ellen's burden, but Ellen needed to know about Oliver's plans for the property.

"I did learn something important when I talked with Oliver," Kate began. "But not about the mystery."

"What was that?" Ellen raised a hand to shield her eyes from the sun as she looked toward Kate.

"He's planning to take advantage of Carol's majority interest in the property and sell it, but not to the state as a wildlife preserve. He intends to sell it to a paper company."

Ellen's face fell. "Oh no."

"I'm sorry to be the bearer of bad news."

"A paper company? They'll turn it into one of those plantations, where they only plant one kind of tree."

"He did mention the wildlife preserve. Maybe he could be persuaded to change his mind." Kate doubted the possibility even as she spoke the words.

Ellen shook her head. "He'll never do that. It's bad enough that Harrington has been abandoned all these years, but after a paper company gets its hands on the property, I doubt anyone will want to come up here for a long time."

Kate could see the other woman sinking into bleak

thoughts. Between the floorboard accident and this news, it had been a distressing morning. She glanced at her watch.

"You know, it's almost lunchtime, and I'm starving. Why don't we go back to the car and grab our picnic basket?"

Ellen's face brightened a little. "Okay. And I can show you the big house."

"The big house?"

"The family home. My great-grandfather built the house here in town. It's where my grandmother summered. It's closer to where we parked at the other end of the town."

They made their way back to Kate's black Honda Accord, its sleek modern design quite out of place in its current surroundings. Kate retrieved the basket from the trunk and followed Ellen in the opposite direction this time. They rounded a curve in the rough road, and there was the house, an imposing three-story Victorian that didn't look much different from Oliver's house in Pine Ridge. Except, of course, that this house hadn't been painted or repaired in a number of years. And as things looked now, there was no hope it ever would be.

Kate looked at Ellen, whose feelings were written all over her face. Even in its rundown condition, the home— and the town—clearly held a special place in her heart.

The big house, as Ellen called it, certainly must have impressed the employees of Harrington Ironworks. Ellen led the way up the stairs to the wide wraparound porch. The house was in much better shape than the other buildings, most likely due to the fact that Ellen's grandmother had continued to live there in the summertime until the family moved her to a nursing home.

"I've missed this place," Ellen said, trailing her fingers along the porch railing.

Kate turned her gaze away from the house and took in a breathtaking vista. Perched upon a small rise, the house afforded a panoramic view of the valley below.

"I can see why your grandmother didn't want to abandon this place," Kate said. "This view is worth a mint."

"Let's eat our lunch here," Ellen suggested. She eyed the dusty porch. "I didn't think to bring a blanket."

"We can sit on the steps," Kate suggested.

They swept the leaves and twigs from the steps with their feet and settled down to enjoy their lunch and the extraordinary surroundings.

"Don't let me forget to take pictures before we leave," Kate said as she poured coffee from the thermos into two cups.

Ellen unwrapped the plate of sandwiches and opened the plastic containers of fruit salad.

"You'd better have something to show Oliver, just in case, huh?" Ellen grinned.

"Plus, I need them for my art history project. The professor's really tough," Kate teased. "I'll take all the extra credit I can get."

Ellen shook her head and laughed. "Am I really that bad?"

"I think some of the freshmen are pretty intimidated."

"They're supposed to be," she said, a teasing glint in her eye. "This chicken salad is delicious, by the way."

"It really should be on a fresh croissant," Kate said, "not

on one of these frozen ones." She frowned at her sandwich. "One thing we could use in Copper Mill is a good bakery."

"Pine Ridge too," Ellen said. "I miss all the little mom-and-pop stores from my childhood. SuperMart just isn't the same.

"What I really wish is that I could make this place here come alive again," she went on, nodding toward the rutted road that led back to the center of town. "But barring that, I just want to see it preserved. If we can't save the town, maybe we can at least save the trees."

Kate couldn't have agreed more. "To do that, we've got to find that will. Does anything you've seen jog your memory about the paintings? Any thoughts about clues?"

Ellen shook her head. "I've been racking my brains, but nothing stands out. I almost wish we'd brought my painting and those photos with us."

Kate groaned. "I could have brought the photos, of course. But I was worried about the potential damage the outside exposure might cause to your painting. Plus, I figured if we don't have all five paintings—"

"Exactly. My grandmother was very specific about my needing all five." Ellen scooped up another bite of fruit salad. "All the clues are in the paintings themselves. We might be able to spot the clues if we can just figure out how to find those paintings."

Ellen's gaze met Kate's, a look of urgency in her eyes. "Oliver has to be stopped, Kate. We can't let him sell this land to a paper company. Now that I've seen the town and the ironworks again, I'm even more determined than ever to find my grandfather's will. Oliver can't act unilaterally if I can prove my claim to the property."

"I'm going to do everything I can to help," Kate assured her. "Now that I've seen this place, I have a much better feel for the history these paintings portray. I'll talk with my friend Livvy to see if she can help us track down your cousins."

"Thank you, Kate. I know I keep saying that, but I want you to know how grateful I am."

"I'm glad to help. Let's finish off this lunch and then take one last look around."

As THEY MADE THEIR WAY through the town one last time, Kate took photographs and kept her eyes peeled for anything that might help her find the solution to the mystery at hand, but nothing stood out. She paused when they came to the ironworks again, and then she walked a little farther up the ridge on a small trail that led up into the woods.

"Where does this go?" she called to Ellen over her shoulder.

"There's a lookout point just a little farther on." Ellen joined her, and they followed the trail a short distance until it emerged at the top of a rocky crag that jutted out over the ridge.

"There." Kate pointed to the valley below on the opposite side of the ridge from where they'd come. "Is that the interstate?"

"It is." Ellen snapped her fingers. "I just remembered. This was the route our great-grandfathers wanted to use to build that railroad spur."

Kate eyed the steep incline dubiously. "How could that have ever worked?"

"They wanted to build a narrow-gauge railroad, like the one in Chattanooga. But it would have been quite expensive."

"And that would have kept the ironworks competitive?"

"Yes, but it would have taken years, maybe decades, to recoup the investment."

Looking down the side of the ridge, Kate could see why Ellen's ancestor had resisted the idea. The task seemed impossible, even in these modern times. She couldn't imagine how difficult—and how costly—it might have been more than a century ago.

"So close and yet so far, huh?" Kate asked as they watched the cars and trucks moving along the interstate. From that height, they looked like toys.

"Seems to be the story of the Harrington clan," Ellen said ruefully, then she looked at her watch. "I guess we'd better be getting back. I didn't mean to take up so much of your time."

"Nonsense! It was my pleasure."

Ellen's expression looked a little too eager to Kate. She liked Ellen, but she still wasn't entirely comfortable with her past—and maybe even present—affection for Paul.

Ellen stopped and looked at her. "Kate, all I can say is that Paul is a lucky man."

Kate simply smiled in response and bit back the twinge of guilt she felt for her thoughts.

She also knew that she was a lucky woman. She just needed to remember that.

Chapter Eight

The next time Paul arrived for the chamber of commerce meeting, he knew what to expect. In fact, he'd spent the previous week doing a little research of his own, preparing for his second encounter with the mayor and his cronies.

"Afternoon, LuAnne," he said to the waitress as he walked through the diner to the corner booth where Lawton once again held court. "Just coffee today," he added. He was determined to keep a clear head. And who could concentrate on anything else while devouring a piece of the diner's heavenly pecan pie?

The mayor, John Sharpe, and Fred Cowan had already arrived, but Paul saw no sign of Clifton Beasley in his ever-present gray coveralls.

"Lawton." Paul nodded to the mayor, then shook hands with John and Fred. "Good to see you, gentlemen."

"Good to see you too, Preacher," Lawton answered, then slurped his coffee before adding, "Guess we didn't run you off last time."

"Was that what you were up to?" Paul joked. "You'll have to try harder than that, I'm afraid, if you want to get rid of me."

The men chuckled, and Paul knew he had been tentatively accepted by the group. He wondered if they'd feel so warmly toward him after hearing the ideas he planned to bring to the table that afternoon.

"Where's Clifton?" Paul asked. He'd never known the older man to be late for any event that included the certainty of food and drink.

"He had to drive his wife down to a specialist in Chattanooga," Fred answered. "Wouldn't hurt if you'd say some extra prayers for her, Paul. Her heart's been acting up again."

"Of course." At moments like this, Paul was reminded that despite a man's claim to power or influence—even as limited as those things might be in a town like Copper Mill —there was no escaping human frailty. These fellows might be the movers and shakers of their small town, but it didn't mean they weren't as vulnerable as anyone else.

"Not much of an agenda today," Lawton said after LuAnne had brought Paul's coffee. "Thought somebody might be leasing that empty store on Sweetwater Street, but it turned out to be nothing."

"How long has it been since we had a ribbon cutting around here?" Fred Cowan's brow creased. "Not many new start-ups these days."

Paul nodded in agreement but kept his mouth shut.

Better for those observations to come from a well-established member of the group. Maybe he'd planted a few seeds at the last meeting.

John fiddled with the spoon he'd used to stir his coffee. "We've been over this before. Not enough people to attract new business, and not enough businesses to keep folks here."

Silence fell on the corner booth, punctuated by the clank and clatter of silverware and plates around the diner. Lawton glanced at Paul, and Paul realized that this was the moment to put his ideas on the table, so to speak.

"I had a couple of questions after the last meeting," he began.

Paul knew better than to start off spouting his own opinions. He'd learned that as a young pastor in his first church board meeting, and he had never forgotten the lesson. Curiosity was always more well received than anything that might be perceived as criticism.

"Ask away." Lawton leaned back with his arms crossed over his chest, ready to pontificate.

"I'm wondering what brings most new people to Copper Mill. Do you gentlemen have a sense of what's the biggest draw?"

All three men looked puzzled for a moment. Paul could see he'd stumped them, and that was only his first question.

"Never gave much thought to it," Lawton said at last. "People tend to leave more than arrive."

"If we get new people," John Sharpe said, "it's not to work in Copper Mill. Most homeowners' policies I write are for folks who are retiring to the area. Or maybe working over in Pine Ridge at the SuperMart."

"What about new industry?" Paul asked. "How long has it been since anyone seriously looked at putting a plant here?"

"I don't know," Fred Cowan said with a frown. "I had to let one of my part-time clerks go this week. Just not enough for her to do. Most of the time, I can get by with just me and the little gal who's my pharmacy technician. It's been too long since there was new development here—"

"Now, wait just a minute here," Lawton interrupted, his cheeks turning red. "I see what you're getting at, Paul. But you don't know the whole story. Quality of life is just as important as bringing in new business. Like we told you last week, we've seen what happened over in Pine Ridge when those chain stores came in. Franchise restaurants too. You can't separate out the growth from the effect on already-established merchants. We don't want to risk losing people like Loretta"— he nodded toward the kitchen—"or John or Fred here. Sometimes you have to protect what you already have."

"I agree." Paul nodded for emphasis. "We don't want to lose any of the local businesses. I'm just wondering how many everyday people—especially people outside of Harrington County—even know about Copper Mill. We're close to the interstate and have good schools, and as you say, the quality of life can't be beat."

"We had some brochures printed up one time," John said. "Not sure whatever happened to them."

"I think they're in my basement," Fred said. "Who were we going to give them out to? I can't remember."

Paul bit his lip to keep from chuckling. These men had good intentions, but like the leaders of so many small towns, they were in a quandary. How could they grow their town without sacrificing the qualities that made it so special? Paul knew there were no easy answers, but he also knew that nothing was impossible with God.

"Have you ever considered creating a Web site?" Paul asked. He'd decided beforehand that the suggestion was innocuous enough to start off with. "When folks are looking to move or small businesses are scouting locations, I'd think the Internet would be one of the first places they'd look."

John nodded. "I just had my nephew set up a site for the insurance agency. It's brought in some extra business, but not a lot. I don't think it would be the answer to our problem."

"I agree, but it might be a start. Do you think your nephew would consider developing a site for Copper Mill?"

"That isn't in the budget," Lawton said with a growl. "Every dollar of our promotion line item has already been accounted for."

Paul took a sip of his coffee. Yes, the budget was accounted for, he was sure, but somehow buying T-shirts for the golf scramble or signs for the craft extravaganza didn't seem like the best use of those dollars.

"My nephew didn't charge much, Lawton," John said. "Maybe I should at least get an estimate."

"Jennifer McCarthy over at the *Chronicle* might be willing to write the copy for us," Fred said. "I can ask her next time she comes into the pharmacy."

"Jennifer's always taking pictures too. Maybe she could help us with some photos for the site," John suggested, clearly warming to the idea. "I'll follow up on that . . . see what we can do."

Paul knew that Lawton wasn't happy. The mayor's face had turned a light shade of puce. But Lawton also wasn't objecting too much. Paul wondered how much further he could push his luck.

"Not to change the subject," Paul said, "but can you fellows give me some advice about a good fishing hole? I've got a friend coming up from San Antonio soon, and I promised him we'd do some fishing while he was here."

Paul had decided to invite Bill Rohde from the tourism board in San Antonio for a visit. Maybe his friend could take a look around Copper Mill and offer some community development advice.

Paul couldn't have asked any question better calculated to diffuse the tension at the table.

"Your best bet's Lone Jack Lake," Fred advised him. "I've got a boat you can take out, if you want to borrow it."

"No, no," John said, before Paul could respond. "Copper Mill Creek's a better place, right where it meets Mountain Laurel Road. And you don't need a boat. Just stand on the bank and flip 'em right out of the water."

"Better make sure you have the appropriate license," Lawton said, obviously still displeased with Paul's Web site suggestion. "Wouldn't want your friend to get a tour of the deputy's office while he's here."

Paul laughed. "Point well taken, Mayor."

"What's your friend's name?" John asked.

"Bill. Bill Rohde. Was a member of my church back in San Antonio."

"Wish I had time to fish," Fred said wistfully. "But those prescriptions don't fill themselves. I'm behind that counter six days a week, and my wife would shoot me if I went fishing on Sunday."

"What line of work is your friend in?" John asked.

"He works for the tourism board in San Antonio." Paul made sure to keep his expression neutral. He'd extended the invitation to Bill only a few days before, although he had a much larger agenda than a successful fishing expedition. That was something else he'd learned early in his ministry. If you want people to truly accept your ideas, you should bring in a second opinion. And he considered Jesus' words in the book of Luke: "No prophet is accepted in his hometown." Even Jesus seemed to understand the value of a consultant.

"They've got that River Walk down in San Antonio, right?" John looked impressed. "My sister's been there several times. All those shops and hotels and restaurants. Says she loves it."

Paul nodded. "San Antonio's done an excellent job over the last forty years promoting tourism and keeping their local businesses intact."

Fred brightened. "Maybe your friend could talk to us about promoting Copper Mill to tourists. Give us some pointers."

"I'm sure he'd be glad to." Paul couldn't believe how easily they'd gone right down the road he wanted them to take.

Lawton had been ominously silent throughout the conversation. Now he cleared his throat as if preparing to deliver a verdict.

"I don't see what anyone from a big city could tell us about our little town. But if he's your friend, Pastor, he's welcome to have coffee with us."

"Thank you, Mayor. I appreciate that." Paul realized what a large concession Lawton had just made. He hadn't agreed to anything, but he hadn't discouraged it as Paul had expected. Paul knew the social code of Copper Mill well enough to understand that the mayor was giving permission while still saving face. "I'm sure Bill will find Copper Mill as wonderful as Kate and I have."

His compliment seemed to mollify the mayor. Paul had some other suggestions he wanted to slip into the conversation, but he also knew he'd pushed things as far as he dared for one day.

"When do you all expect Clifton to be back from Chattanooga?" Paul asked. "I'd like to drop by and see him and his wife, let them know we're thinking of them."

"I expect they'll be back by midafternoon," Fred said. "Appreciate you seeing about them, Preacher. Clifton's pretty private, but this thing with his wife's got him shook up."

The rest of the meeting was spent catching up on community news and spinning yarns. By the time Paul left the diner, he was feeling satisfied. He and Kate had moved to Copper Mill so that he could be more involved with people and less involved with the programming and administration that a large church required. And although working with people one-on-one might be more difficult, he found it much more rewarding.

Yes, life in Copper Mill was good. He just wanted to help make it a little better. And Bill Rohde might just be the key to accomplishing that.

Chapter Nine

So do you think you can help me, Livvy?" Kate stood beside the reference desk at the Copper Mill Public Library. Livvy Jenner was Kate's closest friend and often played Watson to Kate's Sherlock Holmes.

Livvy tucked a wayward strand of auburn hair behind her ear. "You have the maiden names of Professor Carruthers' cousins, so that's a start. Let's see what we can do."

The pair settled in behind a computer terminal. It was a few minutes before the library closed, so no one was around. Kate had warned Paul that dinner would probably be late that night. With any luck, though, it wouldn't be delayed too long. The Internet certainly came in handy for tracking down information.

Livvy typed the first name into the search engine and then hit the Enter key.

"Over thirty thousand results," she said, grimacing. "There must be tons of Anne Harringtons out there. Your professor doesn't know where any of her cousins live?"

"She's been estranged from that side of the family for years."

Livvy paused. "Couldn't she just ask her cousin Carol Coats? Doesn't she live over in Pine Ridge?"

Kate quickly filled Livvy in on the contentious history of the Harrington clan, the nature of Carol's marriage, and what Ellen had told her about her reluctance to approach Oliver. "If word somehow got back around to Oliver Coats about the possibility of Ellen's grandfather having a second will . . . well, let's just say I don't see him acting against his own self-interest."

"Okay then." Livvy turned back to the computer. "Maybe we can narrow these down."

But her efforts proved fruitless. An hour later, they were no closer to finding any of Ellen's long-lost relatives than they'd been when they started.

"I don't get it," Livvy said. "I'm usually pretty good at this. It's as if they've all disappeared into thin air."

"What about the reference room?" Kate asked. "Do you think there could be any information in there, in old county records perhaps?"

"That's the next logical step."

Livvy led the way to the designated room on the second floor. As with most small-town libraries, Livvy maintained a special section for those patrons who came to do genealogical research. Although the availability of the Internet had diminished the demand for the room's treasures, it still had its fair share of visitors.

"We can try some of these." Livvy began to pull some volumes from the shelves.

Kate examined the titles. Cemetery records. Birth records. "This could take a while, huh?"

Livvy grinned. "That's why they call it research. You search and then search again."

Between the two of them, though, they managed to work their way through the pile of books at a good clip. But as with the Internet search, their efforts didn't yield much fruit.

"Is your professor sure these people actually exist?" Livvy asked. She glanced up at the clock. It was almost six thirty. "Danny and the boys are going to be expecting me. Can we finish this up tomorrow?"

"Of course. I didn't mean to keep you so late." Kate held up the volume she'd been perusing. "I never thought I'd find *Death Records of Harrington County* to be such a page-turner."

Livvy laughed. "It's amazing what a little time in the library will do for your perspective," she teased.

One by one, she returned the books they'd been using to the shelves. "Of course, as with anything in life, motivation is everything."

Kate joined in Livvy's laughter, and they left the research room.

"If we don't turn up anything here at the library, do you have any suggestions for where I should go next?" Kate asked. "If we can't find any records of Ellen's cousins, surely someone around here would remember them. Can't we take advantage of oral history?"

"Does she have an older relative still living?"

"I don't think so. Do you know of someone I might talk to? Someone who's lived in the area a long time?"

Livvy laughed. "Well, that would be almost everyone in Copper Mill, Kate."

"Okay, okay." Kate held up her hands in mock surrender. "Sorry. I guess that was a little too obvious."

Livvy's brow furrowed. "Though now that you mention it, what about Old Man Parsons? He probably knows more about the area and the people than anyone around."

Kate grimaced. Joshua Parsons wasn't the most pleasant person in Copper Mill, but Livvy was right. He seemed to know everyone and everybody who had ever passed through Harrington County. He was in his nineties, which meant he'd seen and heard about a lot of the history of the place.

"It's worth a shot," Livvy said. She led Kate toward the library's main exit. "Take some cookies or a pie with you when you go visit him, and I bet he'll talk up a storm."

"That's what I'm afraid of."

"I'll keep looking," Livvy promised her. "But Old Man Parsons may be your best bet."

She and Livvy said their good-nights, and Kate headed for her car, mentally going over her to-do list. If she wasn't careful, her extracurricular sleuthing activities were going to overshadow her new academic pursuits, not to mention the rest of her already busy life. Even so, once she started to unravel a mystery, there was no way she could stop until she solved it. She'd have to remember that when she went to talk with Joshua Parsons.

KATE TOOK LIVVY'S ADVICE and arrived at Old Man Parsons' house the following day bearing a freshly made peach pie and a thermos of coffee. Joshua met Kate at the front door with a look of suspicion, but the aroma of peaches seemed to sway him in favor of allowing her inside.

"Thank you for agreeing to speak with me," Kate said in her best preacher's-wife voice. "I really appreciate it."

Joshua harrumphed, then led her into the small living room. But instead of inviting her to sit down, he walked through a doorway at the far end of the room. Kate wasn't sure if she was supposed to follow him but decided she might as well.

As it turned out, Old Man Parsons had made the ninety-three-year-old equivalent of a beeline for the kitchen and had begun pulling out plates, forks, and coffee cups.

"Set those things on the counter there," he instructed Kate in a thin, reedy voice. "Then you can dish it up."

Kate swallowed back the retort that sprang to her lips. "I hope you like peach pie," she said with all the sweetness she could muster. She took the foil off the pie tin and reached for the knife that Joshua had laid on the counter. "Big piece or small piece?"

"About there," he almost snapped, using his forefinger to indicate about a third of the pie. Kate could only pray the man wasn't diabetic, because that much pie might cause some kind of medical emergency.

"There you go." Kate hefted the giant slice onto the plate he'd provided and then cut a much smaller piece for herself. "Coffee?" she asked.

The old man harrumphed once more, which Kate took for consent.

She twisted open the thermos and poured out two

steaming cups of coffee. "I didn't bring any cream or sugar," she said apologetically.

"Drink it black." Joshua scowled. "No need to doctor it up with that other fool stuff."

"No, I guess not," Kate said, secretly wishing she'd remembered to slip a few packets of sweetener into her handbag. "Where shall we sit?"

"Sit? Oh." He nodded toward a card table and two folding chairs in the corner of the kitchen. "Over there, I reckon."

Kate took her cup and plate and moved to sit at the rickety table. She prayed the ancient chair wouldn't collapse under her weight. Joshua settled in across from her. He took his first bite of pie, then paused for a long moment. Kate stifled a smile at the sight of the older man's ecstasy. Yes, peach had been a good choice.

"So? Why did you want to see me, Kate?" He chewed, then swallowed his bite of pie. "You're buttering me up for some reason," he said with all the shrewdness of someone who'd lived as many years as he had.

Kate appreciated his bluntness . . . in this instance, at least. "I wanted to ask you if you remembered much about the Harrington family that used to run the ironworks on High Hoot Ridge." She figured he might have actually known some of the key players in the family squabble.

"The ironworks?" He looked up from his pie in surprise. "Haven't heard anybody mention that place in a long time." His eyes grew hazy as he seemed to search his memory. "A shame that company went under. Cost a lot of good people their jobs."

"It is a shame." Kate nodded sympathetically. "I'm trying to locate some members of the family," she said between bites of pie. "One of their cousins is looking for them."

Joshua's fork paused in midair. "You're helping that weasel Oliver Coats?" He looked skeptically at the pie, as if questioning Kate's trustworthiness now that he thought she might be in league with Coats. "Rumor has it he's going to sell out to a big paper company."

"I'm actually helping Ellen Harrington Carruthers. Oliver's wife Carol is Ellen's cousin."

"Why doesn't she just ask him where her people are?" Then he stopped and frowned. " 'Course, Oliver hasn't ever helped anybody but himself much. Leastwise, not that I ever heard."

"I'm afraid Ellen and Oliver aren't on very good terms, Mr. Parsons. She's trying to locate her cousins Anne and Elizabeth, or 'Betsy,' Harrington, but she couldn't remember either of their married names. I was hoping you might know."

Old Man Parsons had another bite of pie and took his time chewing and swallowing. Finally, he said, "I might be able to help."

"Do you know where I might find them?" Kate couldn't believe her luck. Maybe things would get a little easier from here on out.

"Don't know anything about their married names. But if I think a minute, I might be able to remember where they moved to when they hightailed it out of the area."

Kate resisted the urge to cross her fingers while he

searched his memory. Instead, she shot up a prayer for God to give Joshua clear recollection of the Harringtons.

"That Anne girl . . . I believe she moved to Nashville with her husband. Met him at a dance over in Pine Ridge during the Vietnam War."

"Do you remember her husband's name?"

He thought for a moment. "No. Tall fellow, though. I think he got a job makin' glass over at the Ford plant in west Nashville."

Well, that was something, at least. "What about Elizabeth Harrington? Do you recall anything about her?"

"Red-headed gal, with a temper to match," Joshua said with a chuckle. "Some fella got fresh with her down at the Town Square one time, and she slapped him so hard I thought his head might pop off."

"Do you remember where she went when she left Pine Ridge?"

"*Hmm.* McMinnville, maybe, over Warren County way. I think her husband was a nurseryman."

That made sense to Kate. Warren County was known far and wide for its excellent nurseries. She and Paul had been meaning to drive over there one Saturday to buy two dogwood trees for their front yard.

"Is there anything else you recall? Anything about anyone else in the Harrington family that might help me locate them?"

Old Man Parsons shook his head, which Kate at first took to mean he didn't have any more information. But then he spoke. "Sad thing when kinfolk can't get along. Always over money." He drained the last of the coffee from his cup. "What folks always forget is that money can be made or lost pretty easy, but family . . . well, once you lose 'em, they're gone forever."

Despite his crotchety attitude, Joshua Parsons was a pretty wise man, Kate decided. "Can I pour you some more coffee?" she asked.

"Nope! Thank you, Kate. Any more of that, and I'll be pacin' the floors at three o'clock in the mornin'."

She smiled as she gathered up the dishes and carried them to the sink. Then she rewrapped the pie and put the lid back on the thermos.

"Is there anything I can do for you while I'm here, Mr. Parsons?" His home was neat but musty, and though he was pretty spry for a man of his age, she could tell that his mobility was limited.

"Well, you could bring me one of those pies every once in a while," he said with a chortle. "Those meals from the Faith Freezer Program are much appreciated, but I don't get many treats these days."

"Then I'll be happy to be your supplier," Kate said with a laugh.

"You know, now that I think about it, I remember somethin' else about that Harrington clan."

Kate's head popped up. "Yes?"

"I was going through some things the other day and came across a few old copies of the *Copper Mill Chronicle*. Seems like there was somethin' about one of the Harringtons in there."

"Are you sure?"

He chuckled. "Young lady, I'm over ninety years old. I

don't buy green bananas, because I'm not even sure I'll be around to eat them."

Kate could only hope that if she lived to be Joshua Parsons' age, she'd have half his sense of humor. The thing about visiting people in their homes, she thought, was that you were often able to see an unexpected side to someone. With a wry smile, she wondered what people noticed about her when they came to her house.

"Let me see if I can find it again," he said. "I don't think I threw it out."

Kate followed him into the living room. Given the piles of books, magazines, newspapers, and other items, she didn't know how he could remember where anything was. But after a few minutes of shifting and sorting, he succeeded.

"Aha!" He lifted a yellowed sheet of newsprint over his head. "Found it."

Kate's pulse picked up. "What does it say?"

Joshua handed her the paper, and Kate carefully unfolded it. The pages were brittle with age, but the type was still legible.

Local Artist Wins State Prize, the headline read, with a dateline from the sixties. Underneath was a blurry picture of an older woman seated on a stool in front of an easel, her hair pulled back in a bun. She held a brush in one hand, and her head was cocked at an angle.

"Read it out loud," Joshua instructed, and Kate obliged.

"Copper Mill resident Lela Harrington may well give Grandma Moses a run for her money," Kate read. "Last week, she won the Jackson-Story prize for her series of paintings titled *Remembrances*. When contacted by this reporter, Mrs. Harrington said that she was particularly proud of these paintings, as they were connected to her family heritage. She is perhaps best known as the wife of Alexander Harrington, whose family once owned the town and the ironworks depicted in several of the paintings."

Kate stopped. "Mr. Parsons! I can't believe this!" After running into so many brick walls, she never expected such a key piece of information to drop into her lap with so little effort.

She quickly scanned the rest of the all-too-brief article. "It doesn't mention the paintings by name," she said, disappointment in her voice. "Or what happened to them."

"Paintings? What have her paintings got to do with finding some long-lost cousins?"

"It's a long story," Kate said with a sigh. "Would you mind if I kept this paper?"

"Don't see why not." He waved his hand to indicate the rest of the room. "I got plenty of old newspapers."

Kate smiled. "I'm sure Livvy Jenner would love to know about your collection."

"Well, tell her she's welcome to all of it if she wants to come and get it. I don't have much use for it anymore." He looked around the room, sadness in his eyes. "People don't care as much about the past as they used to. Now it seems more of a nuisance than anything."

Kate opened her mouth to correct him and then stopped. Perhaps he was right. Certainly her trip with

Ellen to the abandoned town of Harrington proved his point. Oliver Coats obviously cared more about profit than preservation, and he wasn't the only one. These days people thought it was easier to knock something down and start over than to try to repair or rebuild it. Sometimes, starting over was appropriate. But history, once it was lost, was gone forever, along with all the riches it contained.

"I can't thank you enough, Mr. Parsons. You've been a great help."

"Not sure I contributed much. But I'll think on it some more, and maybe somethin' else will come to me."

"I'll check back with you soon."

"Soon?"

"Didn't you say you would need more pie?" Kate teased him.

Old Man Parsons brightened considerably, his eyes alight with a bit of a sparkle beneath his bushy brows. "Yes, I guess I did."

Kate moved toward the door. "I'll bring you that pie real soon, okay?"

"All right. Drive safe."

"Will do." Kate waved good-bye and headed for her car, the newspaper tucked underneath her arm.

True, she'd hoped for more information about Ellen's cousins, but the newspaper had been a real find. Plus, she could use it in her class project. All in all, she decided, it had been worth the pie, and she drove home whistling one of her favorite hymns.

Chapter Ten

While Old Man Parsons hadn't been able to remember the married names of Ellen's cousins, he had given Kate inspiration. The next morning, she made a stop at two cemeteries, the one in Pine Ridge and then back home in Copper Mill. Then she headed back to the library to see Livvy.

"We didn't check the obituaries," she said. "I bet if we could find the one for Ellen's grandmother, we might find the names of the cousins. They usually list the living relatives of the deceased."

Livvy slapped her palm against her forehead. "I can't believe I didn't think of that."

"Well, you have to let me be the one to think of stuff every now and then so I don't get an inferiority complex," Kate teased.

Livvy raised one eyebrow, skeptical. "A complex? You? Not a chance."

They both laughed, and Kate was reminded how grateful she was for Livvy's friendship. When she and Paul had first moved to Copper Mill, she'd been afraid she wouldn't make friends the way she had in San Antonio. Fortunately, Livvy had been among the first people Kate had met, and they'd been close friends ever since.

"Let's head for the microfiche," Livvy suggested.

While fancier, better-funded libraries might have converted the archives of the town newspaper to digital format, the Copper Mill Public Library still used the antiquated storage system. The small sheets of black film looked like miniature X-rays. Livvy flipped through the files.

"Smart of you to think of swinging by the cemeteries to get the dates. Otherwise, we'd have been looking through this stuff for hours."

"Thank you, ma'am," Kate said with a mock bow.

Livvy leaned closer to the microfiche reader so she could see the screen more clearly.

"Here's something." She paused and read some of the text before stepping back and letting Kate have a turn. "What do you think?"

Kate stepped forward and peered at the screen. There was Lela Harrington's obituary from the *Copper Mill Chronicle*. Kate quickly scanned the information, noting Ellen's name among the grandchildren.

"Here it is," she said. "The other cousins are Anne Harrington Todd of Brentwood and Elizabeth Harrington Sweazy of McMinnville."

"Fantastic! A little more Googling, and we're in business. Which cousin do you want to start with?" Livvy asked.

Kate considered the question. "Might as well do it alphabetically. Let's start with Anne in Brentwood."

"You got it," Livvy said.

Together, they headed back to the computer terminals to find contact information for Ellen's long-lost cousins.

OFTEN, WHEN PAUL needed time away and some spiritual direction, he visited his mentor, Nehemiah Jacobs. But Nehemiah lived in an assisted living facility in Chattanooga, and Paul had little time to spare, because his next chamber meeting was quickly approaching. He knew there was no better substitute for Nehemiah than his good friend Sam Gorman, owner of the Mercantile. Sam also happened to be the choir director and organist at Faith Briar Church, so Paul knew Sam's opinions would be spiritually tempered as well as practical.

To gain entry to the Mercantile, though, Paul first had to run the gauntlet of retirees who congregated on the porch every day to drink coffee and chat. Like a scene out of a Norman Rockwell painting, some of the men even whittled as they sat on the rockers outside the Mercantile telling tall tales and swapping jokes.

Clifton Beasley was sitting in the center of the group when Paul climbed the steps.

"Morning, Clifton." Paul hadn't had a chance to speak to the older man or to call on his wife since her visit to the doctor in Chattanooga. "How are you today?"

Clifton was usually full of ornery energy, but that particular morning he looked weary, and his features were pale and drawn. "Mornin', Preacher," he said halfheartedly.

The other men, as if sensing Clifton's need for privacy, moved to the rockers on the other side of the porch or drifted back inside the Mercantile to refill their coffee cups.

"How's Ida Mae doing?" Paul asked as he took a seat next to Clifton. "We missed you at the last chamber meeting."

"Her heart's been givin' her trouble again. Out of rhythm, the doc said. They want her to come in next Thursday for a procedure."

Paul put a hand on Clifton's shoulder. "Sometimes this kind of thing is harder on the spouse than on the patient. Kate and I will be praying for her. Will she be in the hospital overnight?"

"Don't know for sure. Depends on how it goes."

"Would you like me to drive y'all down there? I'd be glad to do it. And I bet Kate would come too, to keep Ida Mae company while she waits."

Clifton looked at him, relief in his eyes. His shoulders slumped. "I'd be much obliged, but are you sure you can spare the time?"

Paul smiled. "That's why I moved to Copper Mill. So I could do what I think a pastor should—be there for the people in his congregation."

"Thanks, Pastor. Ida Mae would sure appreciate it, especially if Kate came along."

Paul would never have volunteered Kate to coordinate the Christmas Craft Extravaganza without checking with her first, but he felt no such concern about committing her for a hospital visit. She would have offered to go anyway the minute he'd told her his plans.

"Just let me know what time you need to go. You can leave a message over at the church or give me a call at the parsonage."

"I will, Preacher."

Paul rose from his rocker, and Clifton did as well. He extended his hand, and Paul shook it.

As Paul entered the Mercantile, he continued to smile. Sometimes the difficult choices—like giving up the pulpit of his large church in San Antonio—proved to be the most rewarding ones of all.

PAUL HAD TO WAIT for Sam to finish up with some customers before he could bend his ear about the chamber of commerce. While he waited, he wandered the aisles, perusing the items on the shelves.

The store's inventory boasted much of what a resident of Copper Mill might need, though certainly not in the quantity or variety one might find at the SuperMart in Pine Ridge. *When did we get to the point that we need twenty different kinds of coffee to choose from, anyway?* Paul wondered as he took in the simple selection of coffee on the shelf. Regular or decaf. Folgers or Maxwell House. No French roast, espresso pods, café au lait mixes, or hazelnut flavorings. Wasn't life complicated enough without an existential crisis over the choice of a pound of coffee?

Sam came around the corner and spied Paul. "There you are. You looked like you had more on your mind than shopping."

"I do. Do you have a minute?"

Sam motioned for Paul to follow him. "I'll have to ask

Arlene to watch the front for a little while. You want some coffee if those fellows outside left any in the pot?"

Paul had to chuckle at the question. He could always count on Sam to be straightforward and uncomplicated, like his coffee selection. "That would be great."

It was a wonder the population of Copper Mill didn't float away on the river of coffee it consumed.

Once they'd filled their cups with the savory brew, Sam ushered Paul to the storeroom in the back and motioned toward a pair of dilapidated folding chairs. "Make yourself at home."

Paul wasn't sure he'd ever sought out Sam's advice between looming stacks of cornflakes and paper towels, but obviously there was a first time for everything.

"What can I do you for?" Sam asked with a twinkle in his eye.

"I need your help, Sam."

Paul's tone sobered Sam quickly. "Sure. You name it."

"It's about the chamber of commerce."

Sam winced and let out a long sigh. "I heard that Lawton snookered you into joining that group."

"And you didn't think you should warn me?"

Sam shrugged. "They're harmless enough. And they always leave LuAnne a hefty tip, or so she says."

"That's okay with you?" Paul was surprised that Sam would be so complacent about the ineffectiveness of the chamber. "You don't have a problem with the fact that the only thing expanding under their leadership is their waistlines?"

"I tried to fight that battle a long time ago, Paul, but I

saw pretty quick how pointless it was. Folks like Lawton Briddle don't want any progress around here. They're afraid of change . . . and the potentially negative consequences."

"But what about you, Sam? You're a business owner. Surely you don't want to see the economic base of this town continue to erode year after year."

Sam shrugged. "I've made my peace with it. I figure I can hold on long enough to get to retirement. Then I'll sell the store. No one but me would be fool enough to keep the Mercantile open."

"But you're the only grocery store in town. When you're gone, what will people do? Especially the ones who don't have a car or can't drive anymore?"

Paul knew that Sam spent many an hour delivering groceries to townspeople who were ill or homebound.

"They'll have to find a way to the SuperMart in Pine Ridge, which most of them are doing anyway, judging by how my sales keep slipping." Sam took a sip of his coffee.

"Maybe the chamber, if it was actually effective, could change all that for the better."

Sam shook his head. "I doubt it, Paul. I figured out I couldn't fight the SuperMart going up in Pine Ridge and tussle with Lawton Briddle too, so I threw in the towel."

"I have a friend coming to visit from San Antonio." Paul knew that if the plan that had been forming in his mind was going to work, he'd need Sam's help. Not just his help, but his leadership. "Bill was instrumental in turning around San Antonio's economy by developing the tourist trade. I want him to visit Copper Mill and hopefully offer some suggestions for how we might bring this town back to life."

"Lawton and his boys . . . did they agree to meet with your guy?"

Paul nodded. "But they're wary, especially the mayor, and it won't take much for them to shoot down any suggestion he makes. I need reinforcements, Sam."

"A ringer, you mean."

"People around here respect you. If you lead by example . . ."

"You overestimate my influence, Paul. Look, I appreciate your willingness to try, but it's not enough. It's like that old joke . . . the one about how many shrinks it takes to change a lightbulb."

"Shrinks?"

"Psychiatrists. Therapists."

Despite the seriousness of their discussion, Paul had to smile. "Okay, I'll bite. How many shrinks does it take to change a lightbulb?"

"Only one," Sam said. "But the lightbulb really has to want to change."

Paul laughed in spite of himself. "Okay, okay. But let's say, hypothetically speaking, that you wanted to try to convince the lightbulb to change. How would you go about it?"

"I wouldn't, because it can't be done."

"Aw c'mon, Sam. Give me a break here."

"All right." Sam looked around, stared hard at the tower of cornflake boxes, then rubbed his face. "I'm going to tell you what you already know. It's always good if you can make them think something is their idea. And anything that reinforces their heartfelt beliefs about Copper Mill would help too."

"I agree, but how do I do those things?"

"Paul, if I knew the answer to that, I'd still be a member of the chamber. Shoot, I'd be the president of it." He shrugged. "All I can do is hang on as long as I can. With any luck, it will be long enough."

Paul shook his head. "God wants more for this town, I'm sure of it. And not mill jobs at the expense of the land."

"I hope you're right." Sam stood up. "But I wouldn't lay money on getting Lawton and his ilk to cooperate with the good Lord."

"I wouldn't be so sure," said Paul.

LATER, AS PAUL WAS DRIVING HOME, he wondered whether Mike Rowland, the young man who was planning to look for work in Chattanooga, had left yet. He thought he'd contact Mike and suggest they meet for coffee after he and Kate made sure Clifton and his wife were settled in at the hospital. He was worried about Mike, rootless and alone in the city. In the meantime, he prayed that God would send a little inspiration his way as to how he could pry open the closed minds of the Copper Mill Chamber of Commerce.

Chapter Eleven

Anne Harrington Todd lived in Brentwood, a well-heeled suburb south of Nashville. Kate left after breakfast the next Monday morning and arrived a few minutes after the appointed time of ten o'clock. When she'd spoken with Anne the Friday before, the woman had agreed to see her on short notice, but something about the conversation left Kate feeling unsettled. Kate continued to use her class project as the ostensible reason for her visit, since she had no idea how this branch of the family might feel about Ellen or the prospect of a missing will.

Kate approached Anne's large home with its imposing columns with some trepidation. What would she find there? Suddenly she had second thoughts about the visit, but she took a deep breath and rang the bell.

In moments, Anne Harrington Todd herself appeared, a well-groomed woman a few years older than Kate. Her blonde hair shone with highlights that were as subtle as they must have been expensive.

"Mrs. Hanlon?" Anne held out a perfectly manicured hand and greeted Kate with an air of formality. "Nice to meet you. I am Anne Todd."

"Call me Kate, please." Kate mustered her warmest smile as she clasped the other woman's hand. Anne Todd's handshake was as cool as her tone. "I can't thank you enough for taking the time to see me."

"It's my pleasure. Please come in."

Anne led Kate through the foyer and into a formal living room. Kate's artistic eye admired the elegant decor, but the room felt more like a museum than a home.

"What a lovely room," Kate said.

"Thank you." Anne motioned for her to take a seat. "Would you like some coffee? Tea?" The woman's stiffness reminded her of Carol Coats. Kate was tempted to conclude that it ran in the family, except that Ellen didn't fit the mold.

"No, thank you," Kate answered. "I don't want to take up too much of your time."

"So, you're interested in my great-aunt's work?" Anne crossed her legs at the ankles and folded her hands in her lap.

"Yes, I am." If the other woman's cold reserve was her customary manner, Kate understood why Ellen hadn't kept in touch with her. "I was wondering if you might have any of her paintings in your possession. I'm trying to catalog as many as I can for my art history project."

Ann nodded. "I do have one, but I'm afraid that's all."

"Would you mind if I see it?"

"Not at all. It's in the dining room."

"Collecting beautiful art must run in the family," Kate said as she trailed Anne, who retraced her steps through the foyer and entered an adjoining room. The walls were lined, like a museum, with works of art from the chair rail to the ceiling. Kate could hardly take it all in.

"Yes, it is a family proclivity." Anne shifted from one expensive high heel to the other, as if the display made her uncomfortable.

Kate wondered what would make the woman so uncomfortable, and the thought made her wary. It was almost as if Anne was hiding something.

"None of us are artists," Anne continued, "at least not since my great-aunt. But we were all raised with a tremendous appreciation for it."

"These are breathtaking," Kate said, almost in a whisper. She didn't recognize all of the artists by their work, but she suspected that the painting above the sideboard might be a Renoir. And she thought she spotted some Degas sketches on either side of the china cabinet.

"My husband and I have picked up most of the collection on our travels."

Anne was quiet for a long moment while Kate worked her way around the room, pausing to admire almost every work. How wonderful to be surrounded by such beauty at every meal. She stepped past the sideboard, and her gaze moved to the next painting. She froze.

Despite the Primitive style, the children depicted in the painting were recognizable even after so many years. Kate could easily identify Ellen Carruthers, Carol Coats, and her hostess. The fourth girl must surely have been Anne's sister, Betsy.

"It's charming," Kate said.

Although she admired the scene, with the bright flowers

and tall grasses that surrounded the figures, her mind was whirling as she tried to connect this painting with the other two in the series. She mentally ticked off the paintings on the list Ellen had given her, and this one didn't fit. What did High Hoot Ridge and the ironworks have to do with the Harrington cousins?

"She painted it from a photograph, I believe," Anne said. "It was done many years after we all grew up. I was lucky enough to have been the beneficiary in her will."

"Her will?"

Kate hadn't even thought about Ellen's grandmother having a will of her own. Wouldn't she have inherited her husband's interest in the ironworks? Had she and Ellen gotten the wrong end of the stick? But surely Ellen would have considered that.

"I think she felt bad that her husband, my great-uncle, left my cousin Carol all of his interest in the Harrington land. So she left some of her work to my sister and me."

"How strange that your great-uncle's will would be so weighted toward Carol," Kate said, hoping to elicit more information from Anne. "Was that unusual?"

"None of us could understand it, especially when he made no mention of my cousin Ellen, his own granddaughter."

Kate wondered whether she should tell Anne that the professor of her art history class was none other than Ellen Harrington Carruthers.

"It's a shame we lost touch simply over money," Anne continued. "But Oliver was so horsey about the whole thing, and Carol wouldn't speak up for herself . . ."

"Actually—" Kate began, but before she could confess,

Anne interrupted her. The woman's cool reserve had melted away, leaving a haunted look in her eyes.

"Now that I think about it, I actually have another of my great-aunt's paintings."

"You do?"

Anne's expression warmed. "It's in the guest powder room. I'm afraid it's not very good, though. Certainly not up to the standard of this one."

Kate couldn't contain her curiosity. "Would you mind if I took a look at that painting too? The more of your great-aunt's work I can find, the better my project will be."

"Of course." Anne led her guest through more art-lined halls until they reached a beautiful powder room with a separate lavatory attached. Kate couldn't help but be impressed. The painting hung above a beautifully upholstered bench.

"You can see the difference immediately, I'm sure," she said. "The subject matter is rather uninspiring, but Aunt Lela was always rather fond of the place."

Kate took one look at the painting and had to keep herself from clapping her hands with glee. After her trip to the abandoned town of Harrington, she had no trouble identifying the company store and the post office. Kate wondered if this was the painting entitled *Progress Comes to Harrington*.

The painting filled in some of the details that had disappeared from the real setting with the passage of time. The sign above the company store was lettered in cherry red, and the windows boasted blue-and-white-checked gingham curtains. Barrels and bushel baskets dotted the wood porch. The painting also depicted residents of Harrington hurrying to and fro. One woman emerged from the store with a basket brimming with bread, eggs, and apples, while a man who was clearly a postal rider placed his foot in the stirrup of his saddle, ready to mount his horse.

"It really gives a sense of the place, don't you think?" Kate asked.

Anne nodded. "Certainly takes me back. I never saw the town when it was still thriving, but in my childhood, most of the buildings were still intact. The sign here," she pointed toward the store, "was only hanging by a few nails by then, but you could still read it."

"What else do you remember?"

Anne appeared lost in thought for a long moment. "We had some wonderful times playing there when we were young." Her eyes held a far-off look, as if she was straining to see memories that were almost too distant to discern. "My great-aunt still lived in the big house during the summer. We called it that because it was the biggest house in town. She'd pack knapsacks for each of us in the morning and send us out to explore." She sighed with remembered contentment. "We rarely made it home before dark."

"What did you do?" Kate wanted to see if Anne's memories matched Ellen's.

"Everything," she said with a laugh. "We knew every nook and cranny of those old buildings, although we avoided the hotel. We decided early on that it was haunted."

"Was it?"

"No. Well, not by anything other than our childish imaginings."

"Did you play anywhere else?"

"We snuck up to the ironworks, even though my great-aunt told us not to. Still, looking back, I think she must have known what we were up to. Maybe she understood how children need to do something forbidden every once in a while."

"It sounds like she loved the place."

"Yes. It pained her to see it fall into disrepair. I think she always secretly hoped that the town might be revived someday. But by then, the iron industry had changed too much. Plus, without a rail line ... well, there was just no way to make it work."

"It sounds as if you were close to all of your cousins."

"Yes, it's a shame things didn't work out." A shadow crossed her face. "And then Ellen moved away, and we lost touch. And I'd never dare ask Carol if she knew how to get in touch with her. I assumed Oliver cut off all contact with Ellen the way he did with me."

"What about your sister Elizabeth?"

Anne's face paled. "Betsy? I'm afraid we lost her last year. To cancer. Carol came to the funeral, but I never heard anything from Ellen. I don't even know if she's aware of it."

Kate was sure she wasn't. "Anne, I need to tell you something."

"Yes?"

"I'm afraid I came here under a bit of a false pretense."

Anne stiffened, and she looked more like the woman who had first answered the door. Suspicion creased her brow. "What do you mean?"

"I'm sorry. Please don't be alarmed. It's nothing very dramatic, but there's a personal connection between my class project and your great-aunt."

"A personal connection?"

"My art history professor is Ellen Harrington Carruthers. I learned about your great-aunt from her, and then I chose her work for my project."

"Ellen's teaching in Pine Ridge? Really?"

Kate expected the other woman to be angry at her subterfuge, but instead, a wave of joy washed across Anne's face.

"I'm sorry," Kate began. "I should have told you sooner, but it was awkward—"

"No, don't be sorry. I'm delighted to know that she's back in Tennessee." Anne stopped for a moment, a frown replacing her smile. "I know it's been a bad business with Oliver, but I'd love to see Ellen again. Especially since my sis—" She broke off suddenly, then continued. "Do you think that . . . well, no . . . I shouldn't ask."

"Ask what?"

"Whether you might be willing to be an intermediary between me and my cousin. Bear the olive branch, so to speak."

Kate sighed with relief. "I'd be delighted to help you reconcile."

Anne's fingers traced the painting's frame. "It's a shame I've kept it here all these years." She looked at Kate. "I'd like to give it to Ellen. Would you be willing to take it to her for me?"

"Wouldn't you rather deliver it yourself?" Kate had no doubt that Ellen would be as pleased to see her cousin as Anne had been when she heard about Ellen's return.

"I think a go-between might not be a bad idea. The last time we saw each other . . . well, let's just say I'd like to forget that conversation."

Kate decided not to press her further. The memory was obviously painful. "I'd be happy to give her the painting. Do you want me to tell her about—"

"My sister?"

Kate nodded.

"Yes, if you'd tell her, I'd appreciate it. I feel so bad. We had Betsy's estate sale several months ago, and there might have been a thing or two that Ellen would have liked to have had as a memento."

Kate knew that Ellen would be far more grieved about her cousin's death than about the loss of any family heirloom.

"I know she's particularly interested in your great-aunt's paintings," Kate said. How in the world could she ask her next question delicately without seeming insensitive? But if Anne's sister had owned any of the missing paintings . . . "Did your sister happen to have any of your great-aunt's work?"

"She had one piece, but I'm so sorry, we let it go in the estate sale. Oliver said Carol didn't want it. Or at least he wasn't willing to pay fair value so that Carol could have it. My sister's estate went to charity, so we didn't want to just give it away. Now I wish I'd saved it for Ellen."

"There was no way to know." Kate wanted to soothe Anne's distress. "I'm sure your sister would have been happy to know it went for a good cause."

"Still, if you talk to Ellen and she's interested, we sold it to an antique dealer in Chattanooga. I can try to find his card if she wants to look for the painting."

"I'll talk to her and see." But Kate already knew the answer to that question. "And I'm sure Ellen will want to be in touch with you."

Together, Anne and Kate carried the painting downstairs and carefully stowed it in the backseat of Kate's Accord. Ellen would be delighted when Kate surprised her with it.

"You'll be hearing from me soon," Kate assured her as they said their good-byes. "And thank you again for your help."

"It was my pleasure." She paused, tears filling her eyes. "Since my sister's death, I've been aware of how quickly life can change. Please tell Ellen I'd love to see her."

"Of course."

As Kate pulled out of the driveway, Anne lifted a hand in farewell. Kate returned the gesture and then said a quick but heartfelt prayer. If only families could remember how important their bonds were, how fragile and yet how strong. And if only they could understand that what bound them together was far more important than anything that drove them apart.

Chapter Twelve

On her way back, Kate decided to stop off in Pine Ridge to see Ellen and deliver the painting. She didn't want to wait until after class the next day to share the news about her cousin's death. She hoped that Ellen would be at home rather than in her office or teaching.

When Ellen opened the door, she was pale, and she looked as if she'd been crying.

"Ellen, what's wrong?" Kate rushed over to put an arm around the other woman's shoulders. She was inside the apartment before she realized there was another occupant in the room. Kate looked up, and her gaze locked with Oliver Coats'. He looked as taken aback as Kate felt.

"You!" she gasped. "What are you doing here?" Kate could see the moment he put two and two together.

"Never mind," he snapped, rising from the couch. "Whoever you really are, I'm sure my cousin has suckered you into believing this wild tale about another will and Lela Harrington's paintings. Are you even one of Ellen's students?"

"Of course I am." Kate had known that Oliver was a bully, but he was more badly behaved than she'd first thought. Clearly he'd been giving Ellen a dressing down before Kate arrived.

"I don't know what the two of you are up to," he said, his fists clenched, "but you'd better mind your own business." He turned his fierce gaze back to Ellen. "You have no claim on that property. Your grandfather left it to Carol. If you try to interfere, you'll regret it."

"Are you threatening her?" Kate demanded.

She couldn't understand why the man would get so worked up over a piece of property whose value was a fraction of his net worth. She had no doubt that control, not money, was the issue. Kate had witnessed enough in the man's own home to confirm that belief.

"I don't need to threaten her. She has no claim to anything that bears the Harrington name." His eyes narrowed. "Don't make trouble, Ellen. I'm warning you."

Kate wondered whether she should call Sheriff Roberts, but Oliver hadn't done anything illegal. "I think you'd better leave, Mr. Coats," Kate said, since Ellen had gone mute. "Immediately."

Oliver looked as if he would have liked to deliver a parting shot but then thought better of it. He brushed past them and slammed the door behind him. Kate put her arms around Ellen, and the distraught woman slumped against Kate.

"Let's get you to the couch," Kate said, helping Ellen across the room.

The woman slumped onto the cushions and put her face in her hands. Kate sank down beside her.

Ellen looked up, bleary-eyed, then reached out to grasp Kate's hand. "Thank you. I'm so glad you're here."

"I was feeling bad about not calling before I came, but now I'm glad I didn't. What in the world happened?"

"He dropped by unannounced. I think he ran into one of the administrators at the college who said Oliver must be delighted to have his cousin back in town. That must have set him off."

"I suspect he was far more pleasant to the person he got the information from than he was to you."

The color was slowly coming back into Ellen's cheeks. "Yes, he can be quite charming when he wants to be."

Kate nibbled her lip, her mind awhirl. "How did he know about the possibility of another will? Did you really tell him like he said?"

Ellen nodded. "But he didn't seem surprised. I think I just confirmed what he already suspected."

"What did he say before I got here?"

Ellen straightened in her seat and dabbed at her eyes with a handkerchief. "He was spreading his usual poison. How I shouldn't be here, how I had no claim to the land. You heard him."

"Was he that angry when he arrived?"

"No. He was pleasant at first. Until I mentioned my concern about the sale of the land to the paper company. I mentioned the possibility of the wildlife preserve. That's when he blew his top."

Kate frowned. "Why should this matter so much to him? My understanding was that he has a great deal of personal wealth. I would think any proceeds from the land would be a drop in a bucket for him."

"You would think. So why would it be necessary to come here and try to intimidate me?"

"Maybe it's more important to him than we think. How much do you know about his business interests?"

"Nothing, really. He's always boasted about his successes, how much money he's made in the construction industry."

Kate nodded. "There's more to Oliver Coats than meets the eye. Otherwise, he wouldn't be so desperate to intimidate you." She paused. "Do you think he knows something you don't about the second will?"

"I don't think so, but anything is possible."

"I'll get to the bottom of it," Kate assured her.

Ellen sighed. "I never meant for this to become a full-time job for you."

Kate patted her arm. "Once I get involved in a mystery, I'm like a dog with a bone. You might as well let me keep going. I won't be able to rest until we get it all figured out."

"You know, I haven't even asked you why you're here. I wasn't expecting to see you until class tomorrow."

Kate stopped to take a breath. In the scuffle with Oliver, she'd forgotten the purpose of her visit.

"I have some good news, but I also have some sad news."

"I think you'd better tell me the good news first. I need to hear something positive right now."

"How about I show you instead of telling you? But I'll need your help."

Kate led Ellen out to her car to fetch the painting. She'd left it in the car because it was too heavy for her to carry by herself. How providential that Oliver hadn't seen it. If he had known that Lela Harrington's paintings were clues to the whereabouts of the second will . . . well, Kate knew the missing paintings would be in danger if he found them first.

"Voila," she said, opening the car door with a flourish to reveal the painting for Ellen's inspection.

"You found another one." Ellen beamed, the recent unpleasantness driven from her expression. "I don't believe it. Where did you unearth this one?"

"That's more good news. Your cousin Anne gave it to me to bring to you."

"You've seen Anne?" Ellen's eyebrows arched in surprise.

"I made a trip to Brentwood this morning. That's where she lives now."

Together, the women lifted the painting out of the backseat and set it carefully against the car. Ellen studied the painting for a long moment. "Amazing. And she just gave it to you?"

"She wanted you to have it. I think it's meant to be an olive branch. She'd really like to see you and get reacquainted."

"Well, that certainly helps make up for Oliver's ugliness."

Ellen paused, her fingers lingering on the frame. Then she looked at Kate. "You said you had bad news?"

"Unfortunately, yes. But let's take the painting inside first."

As a pastor's wife, Kate had more than her share of experience at delivering such sad tidings. She shot a quick prayer heavenward as the women carried the painting into Ellen's apartment. They set it on the mantel in the dining room and gazed at it for a while, then Kate decided it was time to break the news.

"Anne told me that her sister Betsy passed away not long ago. Cancer, she said."

"Oh." Ellen's eyes filled. "I'm very sorry to hear that. Betsy was always the instigator when we got into mischief." She sniffed and wiped at her tears with the tip of a finger. "You would have liked her. Everyone did."

"Why don't I fix you a cup of tea?" Kate suggested. "You look as if you could use it. And then we'll sit, and you can tell me about Betsy. Sometimes talking about the person helps."

Ellen gave her a watery smile. "I thought I was supposed to be the teacher, the one in charge, but our roles have certainly reversed."

"Oh no." Kate dismissed Ellen's comment with a wave of her hand. "I'm just . . . well . . . I'm just being a friend."

Ellen's comment had the opposite effect from what she'd probably intended. Once again, Kate felt guilty for worrying about the picture of Paul on Ellen's chest of drawers.

Ellen gave Kate a quick hug. "You know, I never expected to like you. I thought I'd resent you or be uncomfortable around you, but I haven't had even a trace of those feelings."

"I know what you mean," Kate said. She might not have felt exactly the same way, but she was determined to at least try. "Now, why don't you show me where the kettle is, and we'll get the water going."

They made their way toward the kitchen, and as they walked, Kate couldn't help but marvel at the strange twists life could take. You never knew when someone who ought to be a rival might instead turn out to be a friend.

THIRTY MINUTES LATER, the women had finished their tea, and Kate could see that Ellen was feeling more herself. Ellen had told Kate several stories about her cousin Betsy, and the first wave of grief had subsided.

"It makes me more determined than ever to find that will," Ellen said. "Betsy loved the big house and the old town as much as I did. She'd have hated to see a paper company take it over."

"Does the painting mean anything special to you? Any idea what the clue might be?"

Ellen looked at the painting again, then shook her head. "I'm guessing, though, that all the paintings will be of the area, of the ironworks and the town. But as to what they mean or what direction they're meant to point me in, I have no idea."

"At least it gives us an idea of what the other paintings will be like."

"Did Anne know if Betsy had any of my grandmother's work?"

Kate nodded. "She said there was one other painting, but it was sold in your cousin's estate sale after her death. Anne had one of you and your cousins as children." Kate groaned and touched her palm to her forehead. "I didn't think to ask if she remembered the subject of Betsy's painting."

"Don't worry. I'm looking forward to calling her. I'll ask her when I talk to her."

"She did say it was sold to an antique dealer in Chattanooga. So maybe there's still hope for tracking it down."

"That's too much to ask." Ellen folded her hands in her lap. "You've done far too much already, Kate. I couldn't ask you to keep on like this."

"I want to." Kate did want to get to the bottom of the mystery, but something else was troubling her, something that would probably prove to be insurmountable. Even if she did solve the mystery of the missing will, she knew she couldn't change the devastating effects that years of infighting had had on the Harrington family.

"Well, I'll go with you, then, when you get ready to look." Ellen's jaw was set.

"We can cover a lot more ground together," Kate agreed. "Let me know what Anne says about the dealer that bought the painting, then we can go from there."

Kate knew it was time for her to take her leave. It had been a long day, and she still had a few errands to do in town before heading home to fix supper.

Ellen saw Kate to the door, and wearily, Kate headed for her car. Surely they could locate the fourth painting without too much fuss. And maybe that would be enough to solve the puzzle Ellen's grandmother had left. For now, though, Kate was still stymied.

Chapter Thirteen

Early the next morning, after her daily devotional time, Kate went to work in her stained glass studio. She'd converted one of the spare bedrooms for the purpose not long after they'd moved to Copper Mill, and since then, she'd been enjoying the dedicated space for pursuing the artwork she loved so much.

That morning, however, Kate wasn't feeling the usual satisfaction she experienced from working in her studio. She studied the piece she'd been working on with a critical eye, grimaced, and set it aside along with her previous three less-than-successful efforts.

"Why won't this work?" she said to no one in particular. She resisted the urge to stomp her foot like a petulant child.

The night before, when Paul had been called away for a pastoral-care emergency, she'd spent a few happy hours sketching new designs. She'd been struck by a sudden burst of inspiration as she'd washed up the supper dishes and thought about the mysterious paintings. Stained glass was, in many ways, a form of folk art, so it seemed reasonable to her that a simple style like that of Lela Harrington could translate to such a medium.

By the time Paul had returned late the previous evening, Kate had a stack of sketches and renewed enthusiasm for her work. But now, as she sat on her stool staring at her sketches, she was faced with the unexpectedly daunting challenge of translating her ideas into actual glasswork.

"I give up." Kate pushed away from her workbench and stood up. When she was this frustrated, it was time to walk away.

"Trouble in paradise?" Paul's head appeared around the corner of the door.

"I'd hardly call this paradise," Kate said with a frown. "Especially right now."

Paul stepped inside the room. "Well, usually when I peek in here and you're hard at work, you look as if you've died and gone to heaven."

Kate had to smile. "Thanks. I need a little humor at the moment."

"It's not going well?"

"No, and what's really frustrating is that I'm not sure why."

"Tell me about it." Paul leaned against the door frame, patient as Job.

Although Kate liked to think she generally kept her poise, she'd never met anyone with more composure—or a better ability to keep it—than her husband. Sometimes, she wondered what it would take to make him act impulsively.

"I thought I'd had such a great idea." Kate crossed her arms over her chest. "I wanted to use the Primitive style, like Ellen's grandmother, in my work."

"Primitive?"

"Like Grandma Moses. Similar to the folk-art style but transcending its simplicity."

"Seems like that ought to work well in stained glass."

"That's what I thought too, but everything I've worked on looks amateurish. Like it was made by a six-year-old."

"Maybe you just need to keep experimenting."

Kate sighed. "I know, but I so wanted this to work. It ought to have worked."

Paul walked over and put his arms around her. "Sometimes you can't force these things, Katie. You just have to let them be what they are."

"I'm sure you're right." Kate made a wry face. "I just wish you weren't."

"Funny, I hear that from my parishioners all the time," he teased, and Kate joined in his good-natured laughter, her bad mood already lifting.

"So, you're heading out for the day?" she asked.

"In a minute. First, I wanted to ask you a question."

"Ask away." She was happy to return the favor.

"Sam gave me some good reminders about how to deal with folks like Lawton and the other members on the chamber, but I'm not sure how to put it into practice in this case."

"What was his advice?"

Paul sighed. "He said that I should make whatever I want the chamber to do seem like it's their idea. And he said that any changes should play into those fellows' pre-conceived notions about Copper Mill."

"That's a pretty tall order."

"Especially since I don't really have a plan beyond asking Bill to meet with the chamber when he's here. So if you have any ideas or insights, I'd love to hear them. I just can't keep watching the young folks drift away and put down roots someplace else."

She patted his arm. "You can't change people who don't want to change."

"That's pretty much what Sam said."

"Sam's a very smart man," Kate replied with a teasing grin.

Paul picked up a book from the corner of Kate's work-bench, turned it in his hands without really looking at it, and set it down again.

"I agree," he said, "but I guess this time it's more a case of 'fools rush in.' I believe Lawton and the others do want to change things to improve the town's economy. They're just afraid to try."

"You know how to lead people gently," Kate reminded him. "You always have. It's just hard to be patient when the need is so urgent." She thought of her own dilemma with Ellen's mystery. Time was running out. If they didn't find the will soon, the sale of High Hoot Ridge to the paper company would go through without a hitch in Oliver Coats' plans.

"Any developments on Ellen's mystery?" Paul asked, seeming to read Kate's mind.

"I'm waiting to hear from Ellen. She was going to call

her cousin and see if she remembered which antique dealer from Chattanooga bought one of the paintings. I'll see her at class later this morning, though, and get an update."

Paul snapped his fingers. "That reminds me. Clifton Beasley called. Ida Mae's procedure is scheduled for Thursday. Can you go?"

"Of course. Now I have two reasons to go to Chattanooga—to be with Ida Mae and to find that antique dealer," Kate said, rubbing her chin. "Maybe Ellen and I can do some sleuthing once Ida Mae's settled."

"Thank you, Katie. I appreciate your help on this one." He glanced at his watch. "Better run." He kissed Kate and left for the church.

KATE ARRIVED AT CLASS that morning with barely enough time to slip into her seat. She smiled at Ellen as she hurried to her desk, but the other woman didn't return the greeting. Ellen's shoulders were slumped as if she was exhausted, and she had a haunted look in her eyes. Kate wondered if Oliver Coats had returned to Ellen's apartment the day before, but she would have to wait until after class to find out.

Despite whatever was worrying Ellen, she gave an insightful and interesting lecture about the work of Louis Comfort Tiffany. Kate was glad she'd taken the risk and enrolled in the class. And although she was finding it frustrating to translate her new ideas to actual stained glass, she knew she'd much rather be challenged than caught in a creative rut.

At the end of class, Kate lingered to speak with Ellen, but this time, so did Dot and Martha. Kate had fully expected the two women to drop out after the first few lectures, but to her surprise, they continued to attend.

"We don't know what to do for our project, Professor Carruthers," Kate overheard Dot say to Ellen. "There's just so much to choose from."

Ellen had informed the students early on that they were free to work on their projects in pairs or groups if they wished, and Dot and Martha had obviously taken her up on the invitation.

"What ideas do you have?" Ellen cast a quick glance at Kate, indicating she'd like Kate to wait, but then she turned her full attention back to her students. Several minutes later, Dot and Martha said their good-byes and left Kate alone with Ellen.

"What did you find out from your cousin?" Kate asked, hoping for good news.

"From what you said, I expected Anne to be thrilled to hear my voice," Ellen said, "but she was quite cool. Standoffish, in fact."

"Really? That surprises me. I mean, she was a little formal with me at first, but she seemed eager to get back in touch with you by the time I left."

"Are you sure she wanted to mend fences? She certainly didn't sound like it when I talked to her." Ellen's brow was knitted with worry.

"I would have thought so, but she was a bit . . . different, I guess you'd say. Did she tell you anything about her sister's painting? The name of the antique dealer?"

Ellen shook her head. "Said she couldn't find it."

Something didn't feel quite right to Kate. "So all we know is that the painting was supposedly bought by an antique dealer in Chattanooga."

"Right." Ellen picked up her briefcase, and Kate followed her toward the door.

"Paul and I need to accompany two of our church members to Chattanooga on Thursday. Why don't we plan to go then? We'll just have to take it one antique dealer at a time." Kate wondered just how many antique dealers there were in the city. Probably not a huge number, but not a small one either. "Time isn't on our side," Kate said as the women stepped into the hallway. "I have a feeling it'll be like finding a needle in a haystack."

"What needle?"

"What haystack?"

Kate jumped. She hadn't anticipated that Dot and Martha would be waiting for her in the hallway. She stifled a groan. The last thing Ellen needed was these two trumpeting her secrets to everyone within a fifty-mile radius.

"Is it a mystery?" Martha asked with a gleam in her eye. Martha was always interested in other people's affairs. Her good-natured meddling was well intended, if not always welcome.

"A small one," Kate said, not wanting to be untruthful.

"How can we help?" Dot asked.

Kate pasted a smile on her face and reminded herself to be grateful for the willingness of small-town citizens to do a good turn for their neighbor. "I'm not sure that—"

"Excuse me." Ellen smiled at Dot and Martha, grabbed

Kate's sleeve, and pulled her a few feet away. "If we have to canvas every antique dealer in Chattanooga," she whispered, "maybe . . ."

But that would mean letting Dot and Martha in on the mystery. Kate stood there for a long moment, debating with herself. Then she looked at Ellen. "They'd have to know some of the circumstances. Are you comfortable with that?"

Ellen nodded. "I'm fine with whatever it takes. And considering how quickly the days are flying by . . ." Her voice trailed off, and her eyes seemed to plead with Kate.

Kate's mother had always told her never to look a gift horse in the mouth. She wasn't exactly sure what that meant, but in this case, it probably had something to do with being grateful for whatever assistance she and Ellen were offered. Kate and Ellen walked back over to Dot and Martha.

"All right, if you're interested in helping—" Kate began.

"Wonderful," Martha interrupted with a wide smile. "So, what are we going to do? Man an all-night stakeout? Dust for fingerprints?"

Kate chuckled. "How do you ladies feel about antiquing?"

"Antiquing?" Dot's enthusiasm seemed to fade a little. "You're trying to solve a mystery by shopping?"

"I think this will require a cup of coffee at my apartment," Ellen said. "I don't have any other classes today. If you ladies have time, we can go there now."

Dot and Martha seemed thrilled to be invited to their professor's home. They nodded in unison.

"No time like the present," Martha said.

Kate resigned herself to the inevitable. Ellen was right. They couldn't exactly canvas all the antique stores in Chattanooga by themselves. Not before Oliver sold the Harrington property, anyway. Dot and Martha were a godsend, even if they did tend toward chatty gossip.

"Should we stop at the SuperMart on the way to your place and pick up some sandwiches from the deli?" Martha asked as they left the building. "It's no trouble."

Kate was about to decline when Ellen responded.

"That would be lovely. Thank you. And it will give me a few minutes to tidy up."

Kate looked at Ellen in amazement. The other woman actually seemed excited to have Martha and Dot as guests. And then Kate remembered that even though Ellen had grown up in the area and was connected to its history, she was still a newcomer in many ways. It must have been terribly lonely to return home and have nothing but memories of her friends and family to keep her company. Perhaps that was one of the reasons why she kept a photo of Paul on her chest of drawers.

HALF AN HOUR LATER, Kate found herself seated once again in Ellen's small living room. Dot and Martha had outdone themselves, and in addition to the sandwiches, the coffee table overflowed with a selection of cookies.

"We need sustenance," Martha had said simply as she unpacked the plastic bags. "Brain food."

Kate couldn't argue with that, although she doubted refined sugar and carbohydrates counted as brain food in the medical community. She helped Ellen distribute the cups of coffee and then balanced her own, along with a plate of treats, on her lap.

"So, what are we looking for?" Martha asked.

"A painting," Ellen said. "One of my grandmother's. It was sold several months ago to an antique dealer in Chattanooga, but unfortunately, we don't know which one."

"What's the painting of?" Dot asked between bites of a cookie.

Kate cleared her throat. "That's the difficult part, ladies. You see, we're not exactly sure, but more than likely, it depicts a scene from the old Harrington Ironworks or the town itself."

"How will you ever find it if you don't know what you're looking for?" Martha was truly perplexed.

"We know my grandmother's artistic style, so that should help. Let me show you some of her other work. Kate, if you wouldn't mind?"

Kate went into the bedroom to help Ellen remove the painting of High Hoot Ridge from the wall. When they returned, Ellen took the photos of Oliver's ironworks painting from a folder and laid them on the coffee table. Finally, she and Kate went into the miniscule dining room and returned with the last canvas, the one Anne had given to Kate.

"These paintings are clues," Ellen said, "to the location of my grandfather's missing will."

Martha twittered, and Dot grinned.

"The nature of these paintings needs to be confidential," Kate added with a solemn look at Dot and Martha—

mostly at Martha. "There's at least one person who doesn't want Ellen to find the will."

"Oh, very exciting." Martha wiggled until she was sitting up straighter on the couch. "Will it save you from destitution if we find the will?" she asked Ellen.

Kate remembered that Martha's book club had recently been reading Charles Dickens.

"I'm afraid nothing quite that dramatic, although it would help me, yes." Ellen gestured toward her own painting. "The scene in this painting is High Hoot Ridge. And that's the old town of Harrington." She pointed to Anne's painting of the town in its heyday. "The scene in the photographs depicts the old Harrington Ironworks. I'd like to save the land from being sold to a paper company, if I can. But we have to find the will to do it."

Kate stood up and walked over to the painting of High Hoot Ridge. "We're still missing two of the paintings. We hope to find the fourth one in Chattanooga."

"And the fifth painting?"

"We haven't quite figured out where that one is yet," Kate said.

"I remember hearing stories about the old town of Harrington and the ironworks," Dot said. Her brow knitted in thought as if remembering took a great deal of effort. "What was it my mother told me?" she asked herself. "Give me a minute, and I may think of it."

"Do you think there's a secret underneath the paint?" Martha asked. "Something on the canvas itself?"

Kate was surprised that neither she nor Ellen had considered that possibility.

"I don't know, but it would be risky to deface the painting," Ellen said hesitantly. "What if we destroyed some important clue in the process?"

"Maybe we could scrape away a tiny bit of the corner," Kate suggested. "Just to see."

A moment later, the food and coffee were abandoned in favor of a small X-Acto knife. Ellen laid the painting across the top of her dining table and carefully worked at dislodging the paint from a corner of the canvas that depicted the company store and post office.

"Do you see anything?" Martha hung over Ellen's shoulder like a child trying to watch her mother wrap Christmas presents.

"Not yet." Ellen worked with painstaking slowness.

Kate, standing on the opposite side of the table, watched with almost as much anticipation as Martha, but she was skeptical that solving the mystery would be quite that easy.

"No, nothing," Ellen said at last, laying aside the knife and brushing paint chips off her hands. "Just canvas underneath."

"Rats," Martha said. "Maybe if we tried in the middle?"

Kate picked up the knife that Ellen had laid on the table before Martha could reach for it. "I'm guessing that the scenes depicted in the paintings contain the clues rather than the canvases themselves."

"And even if the clues were somehow concealed underneath the paint," Ellen said, "I must admit I'm not willing to destroy the paintings for the will." Her sentiment matched Kate's exactly.

"We've got to find those two missing paintings so we can connect the remaining pieces of the puzzle," Kate said. "We want to go to Chattanooga on Thursday to start looking."

"We can help," Dot offered. "Divide and conquer, you know."

Kate looked at Ellen, and they had to smile at each other. "We were hoping you might be willing to do that," Kate said. "The painting we're looking for would fit the same general subject matter of one of these paintings, but as we said, we don't know exactly what it will look like."

"I'll pack sandwiches," Martha said with enthusiasm.

"Oh no. Lunch will be my treat," Ellen said. "I'm grateful for your help." She looked at the three women. "I'd never have imagined taking a field trip quite like this with my students."

"I'll print out photos of all three paintings for each of us to carry," Kate offered. "That should help us as we're searching."

Plans in place, the foursome finished their coffee and treats, then Kate and the others gathered up their purses and leftovers before bidding Ellen good-bye.

On her way home, Kate had to laugh to herself about the strange turn of events. The last thing she'd thought would happen in puzzling out this mystery was that she'd end up in cahoots with Dot Bagley and Martha Sinclair. But she was grateful for their help, grateful for the camaraderie of small-town life, and grateful that she wouldn't be searching every antique store in Chattanooga on her own.

Chapter Fourteen

The caravan of cars that departed Copper Mill for Chattanooga one misty late September morning contained a rather eclectic collection of occupants. Paul was driving Clifton Beasley's Buick sedan, with Clifton in the front seat and Ida Mae in the rear. Kate followed in her Accord with Dot and Martha. Ellen brought up the rear in her economical compact since she thought she might stay overnight if they failed to locate the painting that day.

Ida Mae had to check into the hospital by eight o'clock that morning, so they were underway before most of Copper Mill was out and about.

As always, Kate enjoyed the view of steep ridges and breathtaking vistas as she drove along. Her home state of Texas had beauties of its own, but the pure bliss of an autumn Tennessee morning never failed to soothe her. The peaceful effects of the landscape were somewhat tempered, however, by Dot and Martha's running chatter.

"Ida Mae won't want all of us fussing over her," Dot said. "I'll go back to that pre-op area and stay with her until they come get her for the procedure."

"She needs her friends," Martha insisted. "And Clifton won't be any use at a time like that. Men never are."

Kate thought she might beg to differ. Paul was a great comfort to his parishioners when they were in their small pre-op rooms waiting to be taken back for an outpatient procedure or surgery. But she held her silence, because she herself wasn't sure what Ida Mae might prefer.

"Clifton can sit in the waiting room with Paul. Once Ida Mae's taken back, we can set out on our search." Dot had it all planned out. "Paul can keep him company. Clifton's not the kind to want a bunch of women fussing around him while he's waiting like that."

One thing Kate admired about the people of Copper Mill was their combination of caring and pragmatism.

"Ida Mae will be in recovery for a while," Kate informed them. "The doctor said to expect it to be mid- to late afternoon before she's ready to go home, and she may even need to stay the night."

"That gives us plenty of time to search," Dot replied. "We have cell phones, so Paul can call us if we're needed."

Martha nodded in agreement. "But I still think both of us should go back with Ida Mae."

That particular argument, Kate noted, was sufficient to keep the two ladies occupied all the way to Chattanooga.

IN THE END, Ida Mae asked Kate to accompany her to the pre-op area. Dot pursed her lips, Martha looked disappointed, and Ellen suggested that the two ladies accompany her to the cafeteria to buy coffee for the group. Clifton and Paul settled into chairs in the waiting room.

Kate prayed with Ida Mae before the orderlies came to get her and assured her she'd be back by the end of the day.

"I'm grateful to have you here," Ida Mae whispered after Kate ended her prayer. "You're a real comfort."

"I'm glad I'm here too," Kate said, squeezing Ida Mae's free hand. Her other hand had an IV protruding from it.

"Take care of Clifton. He's not much good at waiting around."

"Paul's got him well in hand," Kate assured her and then waved as the orderlies wheeled Ida Mae out of the room. While solving mysteries was important to Kate, caring for others would *always* come first.

By midmorning, the women were off on their search. Paul promised to call them the minute he and Clifton heard anything from the doctor. Dot had found Clifton a fishing magazine, and Paul had brought a Bible commentary to take notes for his upcoming sermon while they waited.

Ellen had used the Internet to identify as many antique dealers as she could and map out a route for them to follow. After some discussion, they decided to stick together rather than split up. Instead, they worked methodically, sectioning off each store and looking through the merchandise with great care. By noon, though, their spirits were starting to flag. Kate suggested lunch at a nearby tearoom she enjoyed, and the others agreed. Then, fortified by a delicious soup-and-sandwich combo, they resumed their search.

The afternoon flew by, and time was running out when they arrived at their final destination. The Rivertown Antique Mall was located in an old warehouse not far from the riverfront.

"Shall we divide and conquer here?" Ellen asked as Kate pulled into a parking space in the lot next to the old warehouse. Like much of downtown Chattanooga, the antique mall was part of the urban-renewal program the city had pursued for the past ten years.

"Maybe in pairs?" Kate suggested.

"Good idea."

The mall furnished brochures with maps of all the booths rented by various vendors. The warehouse-sized room, filled to the brim with furniture and collectibles, looked as if an antique tornado had hit it. Each individual booth had its own personality, from elegant to kitschy.

The mall had a central hallway, with the booths flanking each side, so Kate directed Martha and Dot to take the right-hand side while she and Ellen took the left. As Martha and Dot walked away, Kate could see them whisking out the photo prints she'd made of the three paintings and arguing good-naturedly about who would find the missing painting first.

"Shall we?" Kate said to Ellen and waved a hand toward the nearest booth.

"After you."

Kate was glad to see the smile on Ellen's face. She

knew it must have been difficult to have so much hinging on what could very likely prove to be a fruitless search. But she admired Ellen's courage in the face of the rather daunting odds. No wonder Paul had liked her.

"Oh, look at this Fostoria." Ellen had spotted a selection of glassware on a baker's rack. "My grandmother had a number of pieces like this." A wistful look appeared on her face. "I wonder what ever happened to that punch bowl and the matching cups . . ."

"An antique Fostoria punch bowl?" Kate marveled at the thought. "That would be worth a fortune these days."

"But its sentimental value would be much higher." Ellen traced a finger along the curve of a blue glass pitcher. "I can't believe how I've let so much of the past get away from me. Sometimes it's nice to have a few special mementos that are tied to your history. My grandmother's painting was really the only thing I ended up with. And now the one that Anne gave me."

Kate wondered briefly why people were so apt to hang on to meaningless objects and let the really important ones get away. She thought of the few boxes still stacked in her garage that she and Paul had packed up in San Antonio. They'd never even gotten around to opening many of them. In a way, they reminded her of the antique mall—so many things that didn't really have much value except to the person who bought it.

"It's not the punch bowl or the paintings themselves," Kate said, hoping to encourage Ellen. "It's the memories they represent."

Ellen laughed. "You're right, Kate. My grandmother always brought that bowl out for weddings and funerals, for bridal and baby showers."

"Look. Here's a stack of paintings." Ellen's voice broke into Kate's thoughts.

Kate wove her way around several displays to see what Ellen had found. Several oil canvases were leaning against the wall of a booth.

"Anything look promising?" Kate asked.

Ellen flipped through the canvases one by one. "No . . ." She looked up at Kate with disappointment in her eyes when she'd finished looking through the stack. "I guess we'd better keep going."

"You know what my mother always said?" Kate knew it would be important to keep Ellen's spirits up as they searched.

"What was that?"

"You always find something in the last place you look."

The old chestnut teased a smile onto Ellen's face. "Words of wisdom, huh?"

"My mother had a number of them."

"My grandmother too."

With a renewed sense of camaraderie, they continued to work their way methodically, booth by booth, down the left-hand side of the antique mall. They were about to enter the next-to-the-last booth when Kate heard Ellen gasp. Before she knew what was happening, Ellen had grabbed her elbow and tugged her inside.

"What's wrong?" Ellen looked as if she'd seen a ghost.

"It's Oliver."

"Oliver?" Kate could hardly believe it.

"Yes. He was coming this way." Ellen continued to tug Kate further into the booth, which was separated into distinct sections by large dividers. Kate followed along, unresisting, until Ellen had them hidden in the very back of the booth.

"What are we going to do? I don't want to deal with him, Kate. He's so unpleasant."

Kate looked around to see if she could find a back exit. Maybe they could duck out without being seen. Unfortunately, no such avenue of escape seemed to exist.

"Maybe we can just wait here and slip out when he goes into one of the other booths," Kate suggested.

"What if he's looking for the painting?" Ellen hissed, keeping her voice low. "He may have gotten the information about Betsy's painting from Anne."

"There's no point in worrying about that now," Kate said, hoping to calm the agitated Ellen. "We just have to focus on finding the painting ourselves. Look, here's another stack we can search through."

Kate had pretty much run out of hope that their day of searching would end successfully, but she nudged Ellen toward the canvases anyway. "You look through them, and I'll keep an eye out for Oliver."

Ellen nodded, but Kate could tell she was still anxious.

"Don't worry," Kate tried to reassure her. "If we run into him, we'll play dumb."

"He'll know what we're up to the moment he sees us."

"You keep looking," Kate admonished her. "If I see him coming, I'll think of something."

The booths at the antique mall weren't individually manned by the dealers. Instead, customers took their purchases to a main cashier at the entrance, who made sure the dealers received their money. Kate was grateful there was no proprietor around to witness her strange behavior as she lurked at the front of the booth, darting a look down the hallway every few seconds.

To someone else, she might have looked as if she were attempting to make off with a bundle of ill-gotten goods. She spied Martha and Dot down the hall, chatting and moving on to the next booth as casually as if they weren't actually on a mission. She ducked out of sight before they could spot her and call out her name. That was the last thing she wanted Oliver to hear.

"Any luck?" she whispered to Ellen over her shoulder.

Ellen was seated on the floor, a painting propped against a nearby chair. When she didn't respond, Kate stepped closer. And then she saw that Ellen was crying.

"What's wrong?" Kate rushed over and knelt next to her, placing an arm around her shoulders. And then she looked at the painting in front of them.

"I can't believe it," Kate said in astonishment. "You found it. You actually found it." A chill ran up her spine. At that moment, Kate heard footsteps at the front of the booth. She froze. Of all the worst luck . . .

"Quick. We've got to get out of here." She pulled Ellen to her feet, and together, the women picked up the painting.

"He's going to see us," Ellen said, panic lacing her voice.

Kate knew that if it was indeed Oliver, they could probably work it out, even with the painting in tow. But she hated to see Ellen in such distress. In desperation, she sent up a prayer for guidance. Then she nodded toward a japanned screen, and the women scurried behind it with the painting. Once behind the screen, they were hidden from view in the sliver of space between the screen and the booth wall, though with the two of them and the painting, there was very little room. Kate held a finger to her lips, and Ellen nodded in understanding.

Slowly the footsteps moved around the booth. A man's footsteps, Kate thought, judging from their heaviness and the thumping against the hardwood floor. Dress shoes of some kind, wing tip maybe, like those favored by Oliver Coats. The steps came distressingly close, and Kate realized that whoever it was stood less than three feet from their hiding place, just on the other side of the screen. She hardly dared to breathe, and she saw that Ellen was just as frightened.

After what seemed like an eternity, the footsteps began to move again, away from their hiding place and out of the booth. Whoever it was walked down the hallway back toward the mall's entrance.

Kate let out her breath in a whoosh of air. Ellen sagged with relief.

"Let's give him a few minutes, and then I'll see if the coast is clear," Kate suggested. They slid out from behind the screen, and Ellen sank into a nearby straight-backed chair.

"Fine with me." She slumped in the chair and put a

hand to her forehead. "I don't know why I came apart like that. I guess I just don't have much gumption left since my husband's death."

"Nonsense," Kate answered. "You've got more than enough gumption. You've earned the right to avoid unnecessary unpleasantness."

Ellen was the first to start giggling, a natural response of relief, Kate supposed, following a perceived danger. She joined in Ellen's merriment, and soon they were laughing like schoolgirls. It felt good, Kate thought.

"I'll try not to do that again," Ellen said, hoisting herself out of the chair.

"As I said, you're entitled. Besides, it was kind of fun. I thought this mystery wasn't going to have any danger attached to it at all. And where would be the excitement in that?"

"Indeed," Ellen agreed. "Do you think the coast is clear now?"

"Let me check." Kate moved silently to the front and peeked down the hallway once again. No Oliver Coats in sight.

"If you want to go pay for the painting, I'll find Dot and Martha," Kate said. "There's a cart you can use outside to get it to the front."

Ellen nodded. "Let's meet at the car." Then she reached out and gave Kate a hug. "Thank you. I don't know what I would have done without you."

"Oh, I'm sure you'd have managed."

"I'm just glad that I didn't have to."

"Do I get extra class credit for excellence in concealment of wayward professors and their mysterious paintings?"

Ellen grinned. "If I can figure out how to write that in the grade book, yes, you can."

"Oh, I'm sure we can figure that out," Kate said with a laugh. "That will be the easiest part of this mystery to solve." She helped Ellen put the painting in the cart and then sent her toward the cashier's desk at the end of the hall. Then she went in search of Dot and Martha.

"WE RAN INTO that nice Oliver Coats," Martha said as the four women left the antique mall. "Such a handsome man, and so gallant. He was so interested in what we were doing here at the antique mall."

"You didn't tell him, did you?" Ellen had a horrified look on her face.

Kate bit her tongue. Better not to give away her anxiety to Dot and Martha.

Dot looked first at Ellen and then at Kate. She pursed her lips. "Of course we didn't tell him what we were doing. We may not be as experienced at sleuthing as you are, Kate Hanlon, but we're not completely lacking in sense either."

"I didn't say anything," Kate protested, but Dot was looking smug rather than perturbed. She obviously wasn't upset with Kate or with Ellen's question.

"You don't have to say anything," Dot shot back with a teasing gleam in her eye. "What you're thinking is written all over your face."

"So what did you tell Oliver then?" Kate asked.

"Oh, nothing much." Martha was looking like a Cheshire cat, grinning from ear to ear. "He happened to mention that he was looking for one of Lela Harrington's paintings, and so I said that I thought I'd seen one at an antique store in Birmingham last week."

"Martha! You lied to him!" Kate tried to sound as if she was scolding the other woman, but she couldn't quite pull it off.

"Well, I *was* in an antique shop in Birmingham last week. And I saw a lot of paintings. I might have seen one that looked like it was done by Ellen's grandmother." She winked at the group, and all four women burst into laughter.

"Do you think he'll wait until tomorrow to drive to Birmingham or set out tonight?" Kate asked when she stopped laughing long enough to speak.

"I saw him burning rubber out of the parking lot," Dot said tongue in cheek, "so who knows?"

"Is that what I think it is?" Martha asked, nodding toward the object wrapped in plain brown paper that was in a cart Ellen was pushing.

"We found the painting," Kate said, "if you can believe it. I think Oliver must have unwittingly brought us good luck."

"Can we see it?"

Kate cast a glance over her shoulder and then around the parking lot, just in case Oliver Coats had returned. But there was no sign of him.

"Okay. Sure."

With Ellen's help, she peeled back the paper so that the other women could study the painting.

"What is it?" Dot asked. "It looks like a church."

"It's the building that served the old town of Harrington as both church and schoolhouse," Ellen explained. "I think my grandmother captured it pretty well."

Even in its childlike style, the painting caught the building's dual roles in detail. On one side, a stream of worshippers emerged from the church in their Sunday finest. On the other side, a group of schoolchildren were marching toward the building, books in their arms and lunch pails dangling from their hands. Apple trees encircled both the building and the people.

"Very charming," Dot said, studying the painting with a critical eye.

"Look at the use of color," Martha added.

They must actually have been paying attention to Ellen's lectures, Kate realized. This must be the painting Lela Harrington had entitled *Double Duty*.

"The composition leads the eye right to the building," Kate chimed in. And then they all froze.

"Do you think that's it?" Martha asked excitedly. "Do you think the will is hidden in that building?"

Kate hesitated. "Maybe. And if that's the case, we wouldn't need to look for the fifth painting." She racked her brain trying to recall whether the other paintings had similar compositions, and then she remembered the photos she'd brought along.

Moments later, all four women were grouped around the photos Kate held, studying them from a variety of angles and comparing them to the newest painting. To anyone passing by, they must have looked a sight, Kate thought. A gaggle of women clustered together in the middle of an antique-mall parking lot, doing heaven knew what.

"I think I'd do better to go back to my apartment," Ellen said at length, "and line up the paintings side by side."

"I need to stop by the hospital and check on Ida Mae," Kate said. "Why don't you take Dot and Martha, and I'll catch up with you as soon as I can."

The others nodded their agreement, and soon after, Kate was in her Accord heading back to the hospital, while the other three ladies set off toward Pine Ridge.

IDA MAE ENDED UP STAYING at the hospital in Chattanooga overnight, so Kate and Paul drove home to Copper Mill together. Paul had met Mike Rowland for a cup of coffee in the hospital cafeteria since the young man's construction job had failed to pan out, and Paul seemed uncharacteristically glum about their conversation.

"I know I haven't been in the chamber of commerce very long, but I thought I'd have more of an impact," he said.

Kate patted his arm. His tight grip on the steering wheel evidenced his worry. "Give it time. Bill's coming next week. Maybe they'll listen to him."

"I hope so," Paul said, but he didn't sound optimistic.

By the time they returned home, Kate felt it was too late to go to Ellen's apartment. She called her friend to see if she had been able to make any progress on the mystery once they'd laid the new painting alongside the others.

"Unfortunately, no," Ellen said. "We studied them for a while but Martha and Dot were so tired that I ran them home to Copper Mill rather than make everyone miserable." She sighed. "I'm not sure what we'll do next."

"Sometimes, when I'm solving a mystery, I need to take a break and mull things over."

"I suppose so," Ellen said. "We can talk next week after class."

"Okay." They said good-bye and Kate hung up the telephone. Whenever she felt stalemated like this, she knew it was time for prayer. Despite the lateness of the hour, she headed for her favorite rocking chair and her Bible. She'd learned long ago that faith was the best asset when it came to solving mysteries.

Chapter Fifteen

The next Monday when Paul entered the diner with Bill Rohde, he could sense the special chamber of commerce meeting he'd called would not go well. Paul had had the foresight to take Bill fishing early that morning. That, coupled with Bill's stay the night before at the Hamilton Springs Hotel, had afforded his friend with some of the good things the town had to offer. If it hadn't been for that, Bill might have taken one look at Lawton Briddle's crossed arms and scowl and headed back to San Antonio. As it was, Bill didn't let on if he noticed that Lawton already had his mind made up about the meeting.

"Afternoon, gentlemen," LuAnne said, following them to the corner booth. "What can I get for you and your handsome friend, Rev. Hanlon?"

"I believe my friend here is pretty fond of chess pie, if I recall correctly." Paul looked at Bill, who nodded in response.

"Chess pie and black coffee. And a pretty waitress to bring it to me to boot," Bill teased. "I thought this day might go downhill once we left the fishing hole, but now I may have to change my mind."

It was harmless banter, the kind that went on in coffee shops and diners all over the country. That was one thing about Copper Mill that wasn't different from anywhere else.

"Lawton, fellows, this is my friend Bill Rohde. Bill, Lawton here is our mayor. Fred owns the pharmacy on Ashland Street, down by Copper Mill Creek, and John has the insurance agency here in town."

"Gentlemen. Good to meet you." Bill was, like a lot of Texans, slightly larger than life. He was tall, broad, and wore a cowboy hat just about everywhere except at church and in his own dining room, two exceptions his late wife had insisted on.

The men shook hands all around, Lawton unbending long enough to greet their guest properly. LuAnne returned with the pie and coffee and lingered just long enough to find out who Bill was and why he was sitting in on the chamber of commerce meeting.

"I've been briefing Bill some on our town's economic woes," Paul said to the other men, "but you know much more of the history and the possibilities when it comes to Copper Mill's economic development. I thought I'd ask you to fill in the blanks."

John and Fred nodded, but Lawton still looked intransigent.

"Paul said you were involved in developing tourism down there in San Antonio," Fred said. "'Course, in a big town like that, you had a lot of money to work with, I'll wager."

Bill nodded as he took a bite of his pie. He washed it down with a swig of coffee and then set his fork aside. "That's true. When you're talking about a city with a million people, it's a little different equation. But the principles are the same."

"Such as?" So far, Lawton hadn't even taken a sip of his coffee since Bill and Paul sat down at the table. Paul wondered that the forbidding expression on his face didn't stick permanently, it had been sitting there so long.

"Well, you have to figure out what your strengths are. What you have to offer."

"Can you be more specific?" John asked.

"Location. Quality of life. Schools. Transportation. The usual stuff." He looked around the group. "So, what are your strengths?"

"Copper Mill's a scenic area," Fred said. "And we're not too far from I-40."

"We're friendly," John said.

Paul sipped his coffee so he wouldn't say what he was thinking—that Bill would have had a hard time seeing that quality given Lawton's behavior. The mayor was still sitting with his arms crossed.

"I'm sure that's true, but a lot of places are pretty and friendly. What's unique about Copper Mill? Years ago, San Antonio had a river running through downtown that was mostly underground. Somebody had a vision for using that river, and after a whole lot of work, we now have a beautiful River Walk that's a big tourist attraction. What's the Copper Mill equivalent of that river?"

Bill's question silenced everyone. Paul had some thoughts on the matter, but he knew it wasn't the time to speak. At length, Lawton uncrossed his arms, cleared his throat and prepared to pontificate.

"The last thing we need around here is a bunch of tourists. Or a bunch of citified ways. Sure, we could use a better business base, but we don't want the kind of change that will cost everything we love about our town."

"I understand your reluctance," Bill said.

Thank goodness he was a patient man, Paul thought. Nothing like being invited as a guest and questioned like a hostile witness in a courtroom.

"What if we took a walk around the Town Square?" Paul suggested. "Maybe if we could see things through fresh eyes, through Bill's eyes, we might come up with some ideas."

Fred looked interested. "That sounds like a great idea," he said.

"My insurance agency's just up the street. We could swing by there," John said.

Paul's hopes began to rise. Maybe the men would at least listen to what Bill had to say.

"I don't need any eyes but the ones I have," Lawton insisted. "Waste of time, if you ask me."

Fred and John looked at each other with uncertainty. Paul had the sinking feeling that his efforts, no matter how diligent and well intentioned, might never get him

anywhere with the Copper Mill Chamber of Commerce
as long as Lawton remained in charge. He had prayed
often over the past several weeks that his fears would be
unfounded, but as far as he could see, these men would
probably never do anything but sit in the corner booth at
the Country Diner, drink coffee, and eat pie. He had also
prayed that God would give him the wisdom about
whether to continue his involvement in the chamber, and
at this point, he considered Bill Rohde his last ditch
effort. Maybe Sam was right after all.

"Mayor, if you're not open to any outside help, how are
we ever going to get anywhere?" Paul tried to keep the
frustration out of his voice.

Lawton scowled. "I wasn't under the impression we
needed to get anywhere. Seems to me we were doing all
right before you and your big ideas came along,
Rev. Hanlon."

Paul knew he must be cutting close to the bone for
Lawton to react with such a lack of graciousness, but
Paul's frustration outweighed his sympathy.

"You know, fellows, maybe I'm not the right man for
this job." He stood up, and Bill did the same. "Lawton,
consider this my resignation from the chamber.
Gentlemen." He nodded at Fred and John. "Thank you for
your time."

Paul had a lot more he would have liked to say, but
he'd learned a long time ago that while venting his spleen
might make him feel better in the short term, it would
cause much more pain in the long run.

He drew out his wallet and left some money on the table for LuAnne. And then he turned around and walked out of the diner. Bill followed behind, which was a good thing, Paul thought, given the daggers Lawton was no doubt staring at his back.

"Give them time, Paul. They may come around," Bill said as they walked toward Paul's pickup truck.

"That's what Kate said," he replied. "But I'm not sure time will make much difference."

"They just need to see the right opportunity. Don't try to convince them. Show them. They'll know what they want when they see it."

"Do you think I acted too hastily?" Paul asked his friend.

"Sometimes people need a bit of shaking up. Your resignation might spark something. You never know."

Paul nodded. "Like you said, I'll just have to keep my eyes open for the right opportunity."

"And keep praying," Bill advised.

"Always," Paul answered with a smile.

Chapter Sixteen

After their near encounter with Oliver Coats at the antique mall, Kate dreaded running into the man again, but Pine Ridge was only a little larger than Copper Mill, so she couldn't hide forever.

When she headed to the college for her class that morning, she felt a knot in the pit of her stomach. Such a shame, and frustrating to boot. She was really enjoying Ellen's class, and she preferred not to have the specter of Oliver Coats diminishing her experience.

Since their return from Chattanooga the previous week, their efforts to find the last painting had come to a standstill. Ellen still seemed spooked by Oliver, so Kate had backed off. Heaven knew she had enough things to occupy her time. But the closing date for the sale of High Hoot Ridge could happen at any time as far as they knew, and Kate didn't want to give up without some effort toward finding the final painting.

Her devotional reading that morning had been about Daniel's experience in the lion's den. Kate smiled as she remembered thinking that Oliver Coats would have made a pretty good lion. At that thought, she tapped on the brake and slowed down. Kate knew, with sudden certainty, what she had to do to move their efforts forward.

As MUCH AS SHE'D DREADED mounting the steps to Oliver's home the first time, Kate disliked it even more the second time around. But she knew he was the key to finding that fifth painting.

She knocked boldly, partly to give herself courage and partly because she knew she wasn't expected this time. Again, there was a long silence before she finally heard footfalls from within the house.

Carol Coats didn't look quite so well groomed when she opened the door. She wore no makeup, and her hair had seen only a passing acquaintance with a comb. "Oh, it's you."

Those words were enough to confirm Kate's suspicions that Oliver's presence at the antique mall had been neither a coincidence nor an accident.

"I'd like to speak to your husband if I may."

"Haven't you given him enough trouble?" Carol asked, her forehead furrowed with worry. Or was it fear? Kate wondered if the poor woman could even tell the two emotions apart anymore.

"I won't take but a moment of his time." Kate decided it was better to avoid answering Carol's question, since she intended to cause Oliver even more trouble before it was all over.

Carol pursed her lips as if she was determined to deny Kate entry, but then she seemed to change her mind and stepped aside. "Follow me" was all she said.

Kate's heart hammered in her chest as she walked behind Carol down the lengthy hallway. This time, though, Carol didn't offer her a comfortable seat in the sunroom or a glass of iced tea. She paused at the doorway to the study where Lela Harrington's painting hung. "That woman is here to see you," she said before slipping away down the hall.

Kate sent up a quick prayer and entered the room. Oliver Coats sat behind a large mahogany desk. He didn't stand when he saw Kate, an indication of the depth of his displeasure.

"I hardly think we have anything to say to one another, Kate," he said, leaning back in his chair and steepling his fingers. "You and my cousin are in cahoots to perpetrate a fraud. But you won't succeed. I can personally guarantee that."

"Fraud?" Kate was surprised, and then she felt a spark of anger ignite in her chest. "I can assure you, Oliver," she said, "that I am not participating in any form of fraud. I'm far more interested in seeing justice served."

"Ellen is acting out of spite. She feels cheated out of her birthright, but that was her grandfather's decision, not mine." He reached for a pile of folders on the desk, selected one, and then flipped it open in front of him. "The will is quite clear." He took the top piece of paper from the folder and held it out toward Kate. She crossed the room and took it gingerly from his hand.

Spidery, old-fashioned handwriting sprawled across

the onionskin paper. Kate quickly scanned the document, noting the date and the signature at the bottom. The text was short and to the point. Ellen's grandfather had left his entire estate, including his interest in the property on High Hoot Ridge, to Carol Harrington Coats on the grounds that his wife benefit from the property for the duration of her lifetime. There were no other bequests. Only the notable omission of the man's sole direct descendant—his granddaughter.

"Yes, you're right. It's quite clear." Kate handed the paper back to Oliver. "But it may not be the very last will and testament of Alexander Harrington."

"You think those paintings are really pieces of a puzzle?" Oliver snorted. "I suspect that hardening of the arteries may have addled the old lady's mind toward the end. Of course, she wanted to believe there was another will. Although her husband left her a lifetime interest in the property, he made no provision for Ellen. No doubt Lela Harrington hated to see her own grandchild left with nothing."

"I know that Ellen believes her grandmother's story." Kate paused to pray silently for an organized and shrewd mind. She needed Oliver's help, but it wasn't going to be easy to obtain. She had to present her case in just the right way.

"If, as you say, the paintings are a wild-goose chase, then wouldn't it be better to prove it?" Kate reasoned. "Then there would be no doubt about the ownership of the ridge."

"I have no doubt about it now."

"But Ellen does. And she might need to speak to someone at the paper company about what she knows."

Oliver's expression darkened like a thundercloud. "Are you threatening me?"

"Goodness, no. As a minister's wife, I do try to stick to the straight and narrow." Well, she did try, Kate thought with a chuckle to herself, even if she wavered a little sometimes. "I'm only saying that—"

"You can call off your stupid search." Oliver looked as if he might start snarling at any moment.

Again, Kate could only pity his poor beleaguered wife.

"Lela Harrington's only remaining canvases were destroyed in a fire several years ago," Oliver said with a glint in his eye.

"A fire?" It was the first Kate had heard of it. "What fire?"

"At a storage building on Sweetwater Street. I had rented it to keep some excess household goods. The fool owner didn't even have smoke alarms installed."

Kate couldn't help but think that this piece of information seemed more than a little convenient. "Why didn't you tell me that the last time I was here?"

"The last time you were here, I thought you were a student, not Tennessee's answer to Nancy Drew. You wanted to see the work of my wife's great-aunt, and I showed it to you."

Whatever Oliver was trying to sell, Kate wasn't buying it. "How many paintings were lost in the fire?"

"Half a dozen or so. None of them were of any value but the sentimental kind."

Kate hesitated. How was she to proceed now? If Oliver was telling the truth, then the last puzzle piece had been irretrievably lost. And if he wasn't . . . The story would be easy enough to verify. Most likely, any storage-building fire had made the Copper Mill Chronicle.

"So you're telling me that no more of her paintings exist?"

Oliver shrugged his shoulders. "They were all divided up between the four cousins. There were no others that I know of."

If Kate hadn't seen Oliver at the antique mall in Chattanooga, she might have let it go at that. But he had obviously been worried about Ellen's search for the fourth painting. That had to count for something.

"Even without the second will," Kate said, deciding to gamble a bit, "wouldn't it be the fair thing to do to include Ellen in the inheritance? Surely she has as much claim to the property as any of the others."

"You want me to just give away hundreds of thousands of dollars?" Oliver looked at her as if she'd just sprouted a second head. "I understand that you're a do-gooder, but I didn't think you were an idiot."

Kate bit her tongue before she could deliver a stinging retort of her own. No one was ever victorious in a war of words.

"Perhaps it would be best if I leave now," Kate said instead. "Thank you for your time."

She could see that her polite reply frustrated him more than any retort ever could have done. Kate tried not to be too pleased at having gotten the best of him through manners rather than temper, but she had to enjoy it just a little.

"Tell my cousin there's no point in pursuing this inane

theory of hers. She should accept that the past is the past and move on."

Kate didn't reply. Instead, she turned and retraced her steps toward the front door as quickly as she could, glad to escape from Oliver's presence. She had almost made her escape when she heard a soft "Psst" from the room on her right. Carol stood just inside the room, half hidden behind the door.

"Kate?" Carol stepped toward the doorway and darted a nervous look down the corridor. "I couldn't help over-hearing . . ."

"Yes?" Kate asked softly.

"It's just that . . ." The other woman wrung her hands. "That is, I wanted to tell you that—"

Carol immediately went silent when Oliver appeared at the other end of the hallway.

"I was just seeing her out," Carol said far too loudly to sound believable.

Kate played along, nodding and saying good-bye. She moved quickly to the front door. Carol followed her, but there was no further opportunity for conversation. Kate could feel Oliver's glare drilling a hole in the back of her head.

Before she could turn back to the other woman, the front door shut behind her, and Kate was left standing alone on the porch. Whatever Carol Coats had been about to say was now sealed behind the solid oak door of the painstakingly restored Victorian.

Chapter Seventeen

Kate asked Ellen to meet her at the Copper Mill Public Library the next day, since Ellen didn't have a class on Wednesday morning. Kate would have to confess her unauthorized visit to Carol and Oliver's house and break the news to Ellen about the fire. Something about Oliver's account of the loss of the last painting hadn't rung true to Kate. She wanted to know more about this supposed fire and what had actually been destroyed.

Livvy greeted Kate warmly at the library circulation desk. "How goes the sleuthing?"

"It's about to be on the upswing, I hope, with a little help from you."

Ellen arrived a few minutes later, and Kate introduced her to Livvy. Then she had to break the difficult news to Ellen.

"I didn't mean to do anything untoward, but I wanted to go to Oliver's house yesterday before I lost my nerve. He claims that at one time he did have another painting of your grandmother's. I suspect it's the last painting of High Hoot Ridge, the one we're looking for." She paused.

Ellen looked at Kate, a spark of hope in her eyes. Kate wished she didn't have to be the one to dampen that spark.

"Oliver also said it was destroyed in a fire at a storage building a few years ago," Kate said.

Ellen's shoulders sank, as did her expression. "Well, that's it, then. There's no hope of finding the will now."

"Maybe. But I know you don't trust Oliver Coats, and neither do I. That's why we're here."

Ellen's puzzled look told Kate she wasn't explaining herself very well. "I want to know more about this supposed fire. It seems awfully convenient. And your cousin Carol tried to tell me something as I was leaving, but Oliver appeared down the hallway, and then she wouldn't say anything more. If he truly thought we were on a wild-goose chase," Kate said, "why would he be looking for one of the paintings at the antique mall in Chattanooga?"

"A good question," Livvy said before Ellen could respond. "Why don't we get to work and find out?"

"Absolutely," Ellen said. "If Oliver's story about the fire is true, I want to know so I can quit hoping to find that final painting."

They headed for the microfiche section of the library and the *Copper Mill Chronicle* archives.

"It would be easier if the back issues of the newspaper were online," Livvy said, "but our small-town paper has never been what you might call an early adapter when it comes to technology."

"So we have quite a search ahead of us," Kate warned Ellen. "Are you up for it?"

"Of course."

"When did Oliver say this fire happened?" Livvy asked. "It would help if we had a date."

"All he said was that it took place several years ago," Kate replied. "Do you remember hearing anything about it?"

Livvy shook her head. "Let's get cracking."

Such painstaking research, Kate decided an hour later, took more patience than she normally had. Ellen, on the other hand, being of an academic bent, took to their search like a duck to water. She zipped through microfiche with an almost scary efficiency.

"I think I found something," Ellen said at length.

Kate sighed with relief and pushed away from the large machine she'd been using.

"What is it?"

Kate and Livvy flanked Ellen and peered at the screen. The headline was small, and the story contained only a minimum of information. A storage building on Sweetwater Street had burned as a result of undetermined causes. Arson hadn't been suspected according to the *Chronicle*. No one had been harmed, and the firefighters had extinguished the blaze quickly.

"That's it?" Kate said. "Well, now we know he was telling a partial truth, at least."

"I was really hoping he wasn't," Ellen said, then looked at Kate. "What do we do now?"

Kate shook her head. "I don't know."

"I have an idea," Livvy said. The other two women turned toward her eagerly. "How about a cup of tea in the break room to help us figure it out?"

Kate laughed, and the tension in Ellen's face dissipated. "Sounds like a good plan to me," Kate said.

They followed Livvy to the break room and helped her prepare the tea. Once it was ready, they settled in at one of the small tables.

"I remember going up to High Hoot Ridge when I was a child," Livvy said to Ellen. "It's beautiful up there. And the old abandoned town is very romantic in a way. I always made up stories about the people who lived there."

Ellen nodded. "My grandmother used to love to invite people up for picnics. She'd tell them all about the history of the ironworks and the company and show them around the town."

Livvy's face brightened. "Of course! I remember her now. She must have invited my family to visit."

Ellen turned her mug in her hands. "I used to think it was maudlin, the way she couldn't let go of the past. Now . . . well, now I think I understand its appeal to her. Sometimes the present isn't very inviting, and those long-ago days seem simpler, more manageable."

"Tell that to the women who washed clothes in the creek and tried to get their husbands clean after a day at the blast furnace," Livvy said with a laugh.

"Longing," Kate said suddenly. "*That's* what I felt in Harrington the day we went up there, Ellen. A real longing for the past, for what's been lost."

Ellen nodded. "Me too, Kate." Lines of sorrow appeared around her eyes.

Kate understood at that moment that while her feeling

of longing that day had been a general one, Ellen's had been quite specific. Not only had she lost her claim to the property, she'd lost her family, in part because of Oliver's machinations. Unfortunately, finding the last painting and solving the mystery wouldn't mend that brokenness.

"Wouldn't it be something," Ellen mused, "if we could bring the town back to life?"

Her question hung in the air for a long moment. Kate felt a shiver dart down her spine.

Livvy looked up from contemplating her tea. "What if we could?"

Ellen looked from Livvy to Kate and then back again. "Oh my goodness" was all she could say for several moments.

"It would be a great local attraction," Livvy said, her enthusiasm growing. "And far less polluting than a mill or a mine. The beauty of the ridge alone is enough to entice people up there, but just think—"

"If the buildings were restored," Ellen said, picking up Livvy's thought. "And the hotel. The big house could be a bed-and-breakfast."

"The old church would be a wonderful setting for weddings," Kate added. She could see it in her mind's eye fully restored with a fresh coat of white paint and flowers planted in front. "And maybe some of the local craftspeople could rent out space. You could even have historical inter-preters. You know, those people dressed in costume—"

"Wait." Ellen held out a staying hand. "Before we get carried away. I know we're just dreaming, but there's one very real problem. The same problem that led to the downfall of the ironworks."

"The railroad line?" Kate asked.

"Well, accessibility at any rate." Ellen's color started to fade. "You saw how long it took us to drive up that ridge, Kate. And the road . . . well, it's not for the faint of heart."

"But on the high side of the ridge, where we walked to the top, it's not that far from the interstate. Lots of traffic down there," Kate said, trying to hang on to hope for their little fantasy.

"Not far as the crow flies, maybe," Livvy said, "but it's a long way down."

"It must be possible, though, to build a rail line up there if that's what your great-grandfather and his brother fought about," Kate said to Ellen. "If they could have done it back then, it must be possible today."

"It would be expensive, though." Ellen set her mug aside. "I just don't think it would work."

Kate sighed. "I guess not." She patted Ellen's arm. "But it was a lovely idea."

"I could do some more research," Livvy offered. "Try to find out what a rail line would cost. Maybe something like the incline railway over in Chattanooga. That's quite a tourist draw."

Ellen shook her head. "Without that last painting, there's no point. If I can't find the will, I can't make any claim to the property. Oliver will sell it to that paper company, and that will be the end of that."

"Maybe I'll see what I can find anyway," Livvy said. "Just out of curiosity. If you don't mind, that is."

Ellen smiled. "No, of course not. It's nice to have people share your dreams, even if they don't have any chance of coming true."

"Don't give up hope," Kate said. "I'm not done looking for that last painting. All we have is Oliver's word that it was in that storage building, and somehow I just don't buy it. I even wonder if he claimed the painting as an insurance loss and then turned around and sold it. He's probably worried we'll find it, and he'll be exposed for the fraud he is."

"Well, if you ladies aren't giving up," Ellen said, "then I won't either."

Kate lifted her mug. "A toast! To hope, even in the face of obstacles."

They clinked their mugs together and drank.

LATER THAT AFTERNOON, Kate met Paul at the parsonage so they could ride together to visit Ida Mae and Clifton Beasley on the other side of town.

"Let me grab that soup I made for them," Kate said when she breezed into the house and found Paul waiting for her in the living room, tapping his foot impatiently.

She grabbed the low-fat, low-sodium chicken soup from the refrigerator, slipped the container into a grocery bag, and hustled back to the living room.

"We're going to be late." Paul was hardly ever curt, and his abrupt tone caught Kate off guard. She glanced at her watch.

"We can make it."

He huffed but didn't say a word in response. Kate followed him to the pickup, wondering if she really wanted to ask what had put him in such a bad mood. Her hesitation didn't last for long, though. They were barely out of the driveway before she spoke.

"Okay, honey, what's going on? You're like a bear with a sore paw."

"Two sore paws, more like it," he growled.

Paul was so rarely in a bad mood that Kate was willing to cut him plenty of slack.

"Aren't you and Bill having a good time? Where is he, by the way?"

"He's exploring Copper Mill on his own. And, yes, it's been a good visit."

"Then what's wrong?" Kate knew Paul well enough to wait patiently while he formed his answer.

After a few moments, he said, "I resigned from the chamber of commerce on Monday."

"I can't believe you didn't tell me. What did Lawton do this time?" Kate asked.

Paul's tight expression relaxed a little bit. "How did you know it was Lawton?"

Kate smiled. "Female intuition." Her response finally teased a smile out of Paul.

"Are you sure that's what you want?" she asked. "To give up?"

"As Sam reminded me, sometimes it's best to know when to throw in the towel."

"But you thought ... well, just remember Mike Rowland. You wanted to help young men like him stay in Copper Mill."

"Yes, but I don't think the chamber of commerce is the way to do it. I'll have to come up with another strategy."

"That's a shame."

"Why do you say that?"

"Because Ellen, Livvy, and I had an idea today that might accomplish your goal. Or at least help."

"What's that?"

"Well, it's mostly speculation and wishful thinking, I guess. But we were at the library trying to find more information on the last missing painting, and we got to talking."

"And that's news because . . ." Paul teased.

Kate rolled her eyes but smiled. "We were talking about the old town of Harrington and the ironworks, and what a shame it will be when Oliver Coats sells the land. So much history will be lost forever. We thought it would be wonderful if the town could be restored. It occurred to us that Harrington has a lot of potential as a tourist attraction."

"Except for the fact that it's almost completely inaccessible," Paul pointed out.

"We thought of that. Ellen's great-grandfather and his brother had a falling out over building a railroad line up the side of the ridge closest to where the interstate is now. If it was possible back then, surely it could be done today."

"And the place would become what, exactly?"

"A tourist destination. With a hotel, a bed-and-breakfast, shops, a wedding chapel . . . things like that. I know it's not enough to single-handedly bolster the local economy, but it would create a number of jobs. And perhaps attract some artists and craftspeople to the area.

"Copper Mill would benefit too. Not just from more

sales tax revenue, but I'd bet that tourists would stop here to see the sights and buy something at the Mercantile or the pharmacy. Maybe have ice cream at Emma's or get their hair done at Betty's."

"You've clearly given this some thought."

"Probably not enough, but I think it has possibilities."

Paul grimaced. "Well, maybe I shouldn't have resigned from the chamber. I might have interested them in something like that. But, Katie, it just felt like I was casting pearls before swine."

"I can imagine. Doesn't sound like they left you any choice but to resign. Plus, the restoration idea won't have a chance unless we can find that will. Otherwise, Oliver Coats will push that sale through, and the land will end up in the hands of a paper company."

"Any news on that front?"

"Only that it looks as if the final painting burned in a fire. But given that we only have Oliver's word for it, I'm skeptical."

"Was the fire in this area?"

"Yes. Why do you ask?"

"Why not talk to John Sharpe, the insurance agent? He might know something."

"That's an excellent idea, Paul." She pressed closer and kissed his cheek. "You're a genius."

"Not enough of one to figure out how to transform the chamber of commerce."

"I'm not sure Moses, Elijah, and the apostle Paul combined could sway Lawton Briddle when he's made up his mind about something."

Paul chuckled. "I think you may be onto something there, Katie."

"There's something else I wanted to talk with you about," she said. "I thought I'd invite Ellen for dinner tomorrow night. Is that okay?" She'd decided that her on-again, off-again uneasiness about Paul's prior relationship with Ellen had held her back long enough. And the fact that Bill Rohde would be present made the timing even better.

"Sure," Paul said. "Along with Bill, we'll have a four-some for a game of bridge."

"That would be fun, but I'm not sure Ellen plays."

"She does," Paul said absently as he turned a corner.

Kate swallowed. Of course he would know that.

"Anyway," Kate said, suddenly needing to change the subject. "Did Clifton update you on Ida Mae today? How's she doing?"

They passed the rest of the drive to the Beasley's discussing what they might do to help the older couple. Kate was glad to hear that church members had been stopping by with meals from the Faith Freezer Program, and Paul told Kate he appreciated her calling the folks on Faith Briar's prayer chain with updates on Ida Mae's recovery.

By the time Paul drove up to the Beasley house, Kate was feeling a little more optimistic about solving Ellen's mystery. That task, like caring for the Beasleys, wasn't hers alone. She had lots of help, plenty of resources, and the knowledge that in a small town like Copper Mill, her friends were her greatest asset.

Chapter Eighteen

Kate sprinkled freshly chopped parsley on the top of the chicken divan, the finishing touch to one of her favorite dinner party dishes. Bill Rohde had already arrived and was cleaning up in the guest bathroom when Paul poked his head around the corner and sniffed appreciatively.

"Smells as divine as a sermon," he teased. He walked over to where Kate was standing at the counter near the oven. "And do I smell homemade rolls?"

"You know you do, Paul Hanlon. The dough's been rising all day." Kate loved the way the house smelled whenever she baked.

"I know it's not easy to connect your husband with his former girlfriend. I appreciate it, Katie."

It was a good reminder that Paul *did* see how she could feel threatened by Ellen. But just as Kate was about to offer a reply, Paul reached for a bacon-wrapped shrimp hors d'oeuvre on the appetizer platter. Kate swiped at his hand, thankful for the distraction.

"Those are for our guests," she warned him in a mock threatening tone.

"I'll have to invite Bill to visit more often if it means fancy vittles like these." Paul spoke with an exaggerated Southern drawl.

Kate handed him the platter. "Here. Make yourself useful and take these out to the living room. Ellen will be here any minute."

"It'll be nice for Bill and Ellen to meet—" Paul stopped dead midsentence and gave Kate a suspicious grin. "Wait a minute, Kate . . . What's going on?"

Kate affected a nonchalant air. "I have no idea what you're talking about." She reached for a spoon to stir the pot bubbling on the stove and hoped Paul couldn't see her slightly upturned lips.

"Isn't the timing a bit suspicious? Bill comes to visit, and that's when you finally decide to invite Ellen over for dinner? Are you matchmaking, Katie?"

"Even if I was," Kate replied, "which I'm not, I certainly wouldn't admit to it." Kate had already made the connection, though she wasn't sure whether Ellen was ready to date yet. But she figured it couldn't hurt for Ellen to at least meet Bill and get back in the habit of socializing.

At that moment, Bill appeared in the kitchen doorway.

"Smells great, Kate," Bill said, echoing Paul's earlier compliment. "Can I help you with anything?"

Kate liked a man who was willing to pitch in, even when he clearly wasn't the type who knew his way around a kitchen.

"No, I don't think so, Bill. Just make sure Paul gets the hors d'oeuvres to the living room without devouring them."

"That's like setting a wolf to guard the hen house," Paul protested good-naturedly.

The doorbell rang.

"That's Ellen." Kate reached for a hand towel to wipe her fingers and then untied her apron. But before she could move toward the door, Bill intervened.

"I'll answer it, Kate. You shouldn't have to do everything," he said with a smile, then disappeared around the corner.

"I've got these," Paul said, giving Kate a peck on the cheek before picking up the second platter and heading into the living room.

Kate followed him and stopped short near the front door. Bill and Ellen stood just inside the front door already chatting away.

"We introduced ourselves," Bill said, turning to Kate and Paul.

Kate bit her lip to keep from smiling. Her dinner party was off to a great start.

AFTER THE MEAL, Kate served dessert and coffee in the living room. Eventually the conversation turned to the ongoing mystery Ellen and Kate were trying to solve.

"Wouldn't the easiest way to solve this be to try and get Carol alone and talk to her about your idea for restoring Harrington?" Bill asked. "Her husband can hardly sell the property without her consent."

Kate shook her head. "I don't think it would help. She

may have been trying to discuss that with me at the end of my second visit, but Oliver interrupted us before Carol could say whatever it was she wanted to tell me. Oliver has her so cowed, I'm not sure she'd say boo without his permission."

Ellen sighed. "Carol was quiet, but a bit mischievous when we were young, so she's definitely changed over the years. Oliver was overbearing when they started dating, and once I moved away, well, I suspected that he discouraged her from keeping in touch with me. I just never thought his control over her was quite so harmful."

"Why is he so set on selling the property," Paul asked, "especially if he's done well with his construction business?"

"Are you sure he has?" Bill inquired. "In my experience, you can't usually judge a thing like that without a peek at the account books."

They all nodded, considering Bill's intriguing question. After a few minutes of silence, Paul turned the conversation to another topic, and the four of them enjoyed the remainder of their evening together, playing bridge, laughing and telling stories for several hours.

Ellen and Bill particularly seemed to enjoy the evening, and even tended to ignore Kate and Paul in the flow of their own conversation. But Kate didn't take it personally. She was just happy that Ellen was distracted from reminiscing with Paul, and she was even happier that Ellen had found someone who made her laugh.

"WHY, KATIE. You wily little fox," Paul said as he helped her wash up the last of the dishes.

Ellen had left a half hour before, and Bill had said good night not long after Ellen.

"Wily? What do you mean?" Kate shot her husband a look of feigned surprise.

"You can play innocent all you want with other people, but this is me. Paul. Your husband."

"I think your imagination has veered off into Overactive Land again," Katie teased, rinsing off a plate and setting it in the dish drain.

"You knew they'd hit it off."

"Who?"

"All right, if that's the way you want to play it." He leaned over to kiss her. "But even if you won't acknowledge it, I know the truth."

"The truth is that it's late, and you need some sleep," she said to Paul. She wrung out the dishcloth and hung it over the faucet to dry. "As do I. It's been quite a day."

"Yes, it has. Especially for the matchmakers in the crowd," Paul teased. "Martha Sinclair better watch out. That's all I'm saying."

Kate pursed her lips at him and then laughed. "Come on. You have to get up early to drive Bill to the airport in Chattanooga tomorrow." The dishes finished, they turned out the kitchen light and headed for bed.

"I'VE BEEN THINKING about what Bill said at dinner last week," Ellen confided to Kate as they were leaving the classroom the following Tuesday morning.

Kate was careful to keep her expression neutral. Why

shouldn't two people who had recently lost their spouses enjoy each other's company?

"You and Bill really seemed to hit it off," Kate said in an attempt to be encouraging.

"Hit it off?" Ellen looked confused. "Oh, Kate." She flushed and then giggled like a teenager. "Oh no. That wasn't what I meant."

Kate thought Ellen might be protesting a bit too much, but she knew enough to step tenderly when it came to the romantic feelings of others.

"I'm sorry. What did you mean?"

"I meant what Bill said about telling Carol about our idea for saving Harrington."

"But what about Oliver? He'd never allow such a conversation to take place, and she's obviously too afraid to stand up to him."

"I've been thinking about that. And I wanted to ask you whether Carol said anything about me either time you visited their home?"

"I don't remember her saying much of anything beyond hello and good-bye. And when she pulled me aside at the end of the last visit to try and tell me something, she didn't get a chance. I wish we'd had more time to talk before Oliver ruined the moment. I'm sorry, Ellen. She never said anything about you. I wish I could tell you different."

"No, no. That's all right. It's the truth. Oliver really does have her under his thumb."

"His fist, more like it," Kate said. "It's painful to watch her when she's around him."

"So you're thinking of approaching her when Oliver's not around?"

Ellen nodded. "I was looking on his company's Web site, and he has a board of directors meeting in Nashville the next few days. I thought maybe ... well, that this might be the time to try to talk with her."

"Sounds like a good plan to me."

"I'm glad you think so. Because I want you to go with me."

"*Hmm.* Are you sure? Carol might be more receptive if you came alone."

"She knows you, though, at least a little. And I think the presence of a third party—especially a minister's wife—might be a good buffer."

"You know I'm happy to help if I can. Are you going to phone her first to set something up?"

Ellen shook her head. "I think it's best if we just show up on her doorstep. If she has too much time to think about it, she might refuse to see me out of fear."

Over the years, Kate had met more than a few women whose every move was controlled and coerced by their domineering husbands. From what she'd seen, Carol Coats definitely fell into that category.

"When do you want to go?"

"Oliver's board meeting begins tomorrow. So, would tomorrow morning be all right for you? I don't have any morning classes scheduled."

Kate mentally reviewed her own schedule. "Yes. That would work. Should I swing by and pick you up?"

"That would be great." She stopped walking and turned to Kate. "I can't thank you enough, you know. All your efforts are definitely above and beyond the call of duty."

"It's just my version of a shiny apple for the teacher," Kate teased.

Ellen laughed. "Well, it's some apple."

The women parted company, and on the way home to Copper Mill, Kate sent up a prayer that their impromptu meeting with Carol Coats would go as well as Ellen hoped it would.

MAYBE THIRD TIME'S A CHARM, Kate thought the next morning as she and Ellen followed a flustered Carol into the peach-and-cream sunroom at the rear of her home.

"Thank you for seeing me," Ellen said to her cousin as she took a seat on the wicker sofa. "I know it's been a long time."

"Yes." Carol perched on the edge of a chair, looking as if she might flee at any moment. "Thirty years or more."

"You look well," Ellen said.

Kate sat down at the other end of the sofa and tried to make herself as invisible as she could.

"Thank you." And then Carol fell silent.

She clearly wasn't going to initiate any meaningful conversation. In fact, Kate had thought at first that she wasn't going to let them past the front door. But Ellen's plea must have touched a responsive chord somewhere in her cousin.

"I suppose you know why I'm here," Ellen began.

Carol nodded but made no other reply.

"I need your help," Ellen said, proceeding straight to the point.

Kate wondered whether that was the best strategy with someone as skittish as Carol.

"I don't know how I could be of any help to you," Carol murmured.

"You can save High Hoot Ridge," Ellen replied. "I know you used to value it as much as I did. We had such good times there, with Anne and Betsy, when we were younger."

Carol's face showed a ghost of a smile. "Yes. I remember."

"It would be a shame for such a beautiful place to be sold for the lumber," Ellen said, pressing her case.

"Oliver thinks it's for the best."

"What do you think? It's your land, after all. Or at least it's your responsibility, since I can't find my grandfather's second will."

"There is no second will," Carol said, but even Kate could tell she was parroting Oliver's words.

"My grandmother said there was. That it left me my grandfather's share of the property."

Carol twisted her hands together in her lap. "You really shouldn't be here. Oliver wouldn't like it."

"Please, Carol. I need your help."

Carol stood. "I'm sorry. It's too late to change anything. I think you'd better go now."

Ellen looked as if she might cry. Kate moved to stand next to her, then took her arm and led her to the door.

Kate was disappointed too, but the encounter had

completely deflated Ellen. Kate guided her out of the house, not waiting for Carol to see them to the door. Frankly, Kate had spent all the time she ever cared to in that home. As beautiful as it might look from the outside, she had found nothing but fear and distrust within.

"I thought she would change her mind," Ellen said once they were in Kate's car. "I truly did. We were so close when we were children."

"I'm sorry," Kate said.

"Whatever happens," Ellen said, "I can only be glad I left Tennessee when I did. If I had stayed here to watch Carol change so completely and the rest of the family fall away, I don't think I would have handled it very well. This is hard enough."

But you might have changed the outcome, Kate wanted to say, but she didn't.

"Maybe if Paul and I hadn't broken up—" Ellen stopped, and then she looked at Kate with horrified eyes. "I'm sorry. I didn't mean—"

"Of course you didn't." Kate hoped that Ellen was only speculating, not wishing.

"I just meant that if things had been different—"

"And they could have been," Kate said soothingly. "But things will always be just what they are, you know. We have to take life as we find it and build on that." Kate thought her tone sounded a bit defensive, but she decided that the situation warranted such a reaction.

"And if we find bitterness, conflict and recrimination in our lives?" Ellen took out a tissue and wiped her eyes.

"Then we head to Copper Mill and stop for a two-scoop cone of mocha-fudge ice cream at Emma's. Then we'll tackle the next obstacle."

Ellen laughed. "Kate, you're such a blessing. You know that, don't you?"

"So, what do you say? Are you up for some ice cream?"

"Definitely!"

Kate reached the turn for Copper Mill and headed south on Pine Ridge Road. They'd tried to solicit Carol's help, but it wasn't meant to be. Kate and Ellen would have to figure out a new plan. Until then, well, they might as well have a little fun and enjoy some well-deserved calories.

Chapter Nineteen

The last thing Kate expected the day after their visit to Carol Coats was a phone call from a distraught Ellen. Despite their lack of success with Carol, Ellen had seemed in such good spirits after their trip to Emma's Ice Cream Shop. When Kate had dropped her off at home, she'd sensed that Ellen was as motivated as ever to find her grandfather's will.

"Ellen? What's wrong?" Kate had barely recognized the sobbing voice. She leaned against the kitchen doorway and pressed the receiver tighter against her ear, trying to make out Ellen's words. "Are you okay? Has something happened?"

"I'm calling off the search." Ellen choked out the words between her sobs. "It's time to just let it go, Kate. It's too late."

"What do you mean? Is it Oliver? Has he threatened you again?"

"It's my decision," Ellen insisted. "I know I asked you to help me, but now I'm asking you to let the whole thing go. It's for the best."

Her voice broke on the last word, and the sound twisted like a knife in Kate's heart. Ellen had been so determined to solve the mystery of her grandfather's missing will, and Kate couldn't believe that she would just abandon the search so abruptly.

"But it feels like we're so close."

"That visit with Carol yesterday . . . well, it reminded me why I gave up trying to rebuild good relationships with my family all those years ago."

"She wanted to help you. I could tell. She's just too afraid of Oliver."

"Exactly. I don't want to put her in the position of getting hurt."

Kate was instantly suspicious. "Ellen, have you heard from him? Is he behind your sudden change of heart?"

Ellen was silent for a fraction of a second too long, and Kate's suspicions were confirmed.

"Look," Kate said, "if Oliver's trying to intimidate you or threaten you, we can go to the sheriff. I've worked with him before on cases. He'll listen and take us seriously."

"Kate, please do as I ask. I can't pursue this anymore."

What choice did she have? Kate sighed. She hated to let someone as self-serving and bullying as Oliver Coats carry the day, but it was Ellen's life, after all.

"All right. But I can't believe you're giving up. I think we should press on."

"I can't. Not anymore."

"Okay, Ellen. I'll see you in class next week."

Ellen was silent for several seconds. "Actually, I'm

canceling class next week. I need to leave town for several days."

With that, Kate was definitely suspicious. "Ellen—"

"Don't ask me any more questions, Kate. Just trust my judgment. Please."

"Of course I trust your judgment." She paused, wanting to choose her words carefully. "Just remember that you do have friends here. People willing to help. You don't have to face anything—or anyone—alone."

"Thank you, Kate. For everything."

The words sounded ominously like a good-bye.

"Ellen—"

"I've got to go. I'll talk to you soon."

The call ended with a click before Kate could say anything more. She held the receiver in her hand for a long time before she gently replaced it in its cradle.

Something definitely wasn't right about Ellen's behavior. She didn't seem like someone who would give up at the first sign of trouble. Whatever was influencing her behavior, the threat must have been powerful. Oliver Coats, Kate was sure. He was the kind of man who would employ whatever means necessary to achieve his own purposes. Well, he might be the most Machiavellian person she'd encountered in quite some time, but Kate knew that love was far more powerful than greed. She wasn't about to let Oliver's bullying ways ruin High Hoot Ridge. Or Ellen's future.

THE FOLLOWING MONDAY, Kate drove to Gorman's Mercantile for a few groceries, and though her errand might have been routine, her dilemma was anything but. She'd tried to call Ellen several times over the weekend, but the phone had rung unanswered. Kate guessed that the other woman had truly left town.

Clifton Beasley was noticeably absent from the group of older men sitting on the rocking chairs outside the store. Kate exchanged greetings with them but slipped inside without lingering to chat. She wasn't two steps inside the door, though, before she came face-to-face with Dot and Martha.

"Kate!" Martha's face lit up at the sight of her. "We were hoping we'd see you today."

"Here I am." Kate hoped the ladies wouldn't be too chatty.

Dot looked over her shoulder as if making sure that no one could overhear their conversation. "Martha and I have something to tell you."

Kate had to suppress a smile. "You do?"

"We decided it wouldn't hurt to do a little sleuthing of our own about that Oliver Coats, especially after he turned up at the antique mall like that."

Suddenly Kate didn't feel like smiling anymore. Given how spooked Ellen had been by Oliver, Kate didn't think the two older ladies should initiate any contact with the man whatsoever.

"Tell me more," Kate said as cordially as she could, fighting the urge to look over her shoulder. The last thing she wanted was for Ellen's private business to become fodder for the Copper Mill grapevine.

"Well, we decided to see where else he might go."

"Martha. Dot. You need to be care—"

"Oh, we were careful. He never suspected a thing. We followed him all weekend."

Kate didn't know whether to laugh or shake her head. "I wish you wouldn't have—"

"But it was very easy," Martha said. "That big Lincoln Continental of his can be seen from a mile away. Besides, he didn't wander too far afield."

Kate couldn't help herself. "So, what did you find out?"

"He's been visiting pawn shops and antique stores in Copper Mill, Nashville, McMinnville. All over the place. Looked like he was selling things."

"Selling things? What do you mean?"

"We're not sure what exactly. Just that he'd go into a shop with a bag or something like that and then come out empty-handed."

"But that's hardly criminal activity."

Martha looked disappointed. "Well, I guess we thought he might lead us to the last painting. But we couldn't very well follow him into the stores for fear we'd be found out."

"I'm afraid that the painting might not exist anymore," Kate said, not fully believing it herself but wanting to discourage Martha and Dot from such potentially dangerous pursuits. "Oliver told us it burned in a fire. He said he lost a number of—" Kate broke off abruptly, then asked, "How many places has Oliver been to since you've been following him?"

"Ten. Maybe fifteen," Dot said.

"Do you think we're onto something?" Martha asked, her face shining with triumph.

"Maybe." Kate paused to consider this new piece of information. "Unless it's the kind of thing he does all the time. And we don't have any way to know that."

"We could keep following him," Martha offered. "It's a lot of fun, really. Yesterday we borrowed wigs from Betty over at the beauty parlor so we'd be incognito."

"Thanks so much for following your instincts. You've uncovered a possible lead for me. But I think you should probably lay low for now, for your own safety," Kate said, halfway wishing she could have seen Dot and Martha in disguise.

Martha beamed, and even the normally more taciturn Dot looked pleased at Kate's praise.

"By the way, where did he go last?" Kate asked.

"Smith Street Gifts right here in Copper Mill," Martha said, naming the shop off the Town Square kitty-corner from the Mercantile.

"All right, then. I'll see if I can find out anything from Steve Smith," Kate said. "I need to drop by there anyway."

Kate had sold several of her stained glass pieces in the shop, and she stopped in from time to time to see if Steve needed more of them.

"Are you sure we shouldn't keep following Oliver?" Martha asked, hope in her eyes.

"I think you've done a marvelous job. Now it's my turn." Kate patted the older woman's shoulder. "Thank you. This may turn out to be just the break we need."

At that moment, Sam Gorman called to Kate. Martha and Dot jumped guiltily, so Kate took the opportunity to send them on their way.

"Thanks again, ladies. I'll let you know what I find out."

"You look pretty pleased about something," Sam said as he approached.

Dot and Martha were already moving toward the door.

"Yes, I am," Kate answered, but she didn't elaborate. Instead, she hurried through her shopping so that she could make a beeline for the gift shop.

"Have I seen Oliver Coats? *Hmm.*" Steve Smith, a mild-mannered man in his thirties, scratched his head.

"Tall man, dark hair?" Kate tried to prompt the shop owner's memory. "From over in Pine Ridge. He might have been trying to put something on consignment with you. A family heirloom of some sort. Maybe a painting?"

Steve scratched his head. "I'm not sure—"

"He's pleasant but a bit on the arrogant side."

Steve's face lit with recognition. "I know who you mean. Arrogant is definitely the word."

"Do you remember what he brought to the shop?" Kate stopped herself from crossing her fingers.

"Yup. I can show it to you."

Her pulse picked up. "If you wouldn't mind."

How ironic if the last painting turned out to be right there in the gift shop along with Kate's work.

Steve motioned for her to follow him to the back of

the shop. Kate moved briskly, hoping against hope that Steve might be leading her right to the clue she needed. After all, if Oliver had been selling heirlooms all over the area, he must have some reason. Perhaps—

"Here it is." Steve pulled an object down from a storage shelf. "It has a couple of nicks, but otherwise it's in good condition."

The cut-glass punch bowl was easily recognizable. Kate wasn't an expert when it came to antiques, but her mother had owned several pieces of the distinctive Fostoria glass.

"How much are you asking for it?" Kate asked. It had to be the punch bowl that had belonged to Ellen's grandmother.

"For you? Seventy-five."

Kate knew Steve was giving her a good price. And if she wasn't able to solve Ellen's mystery, at least she could return her grandmother's punch bowl. "I'd like to purchase it."

"Sure thing."

While Steve wrote up the ticket and ran Kate's credit card, Kate did a quick inventory to see if any more of her own pieces had sold. She thought she noticed a couple that were gone. Of course, she'd know more at the end of the month when Steve sent out receipts to all the artists and artisans whose work he carried.

"I wrapped it up for you." Steve appeared at her side carrying a good-sized box. "That should protect it until you get it home."

"Thank you. You've been a great help."

Steve smiled. "It's just a punch bowl. By the way, I hope you're hard at work. I'm going to need some more of your pieces before too long."

Kate thought of her recent sad attempts at her craft. "It may be a little while," she warned him. "I seem to have hit an artistic snag." She reached for the box, and Steve handed it over.

"I'm sure you'll work through it. You're too talented not to," he said with a wink.

Kate laughed. "I appreciate your vote of confidence. And thank you again for the punch bowl."

"Always happy to help."

Steve opened the door for Kate. Burdened as she was with the large box, she almost ran over John Sharpe on the sidewalk outside the gift shop.

"Kate!" He smiled, clearly pleased to see her, but then his face clouded over.

Kate suspected that he was thinking about Paul's abrupt resignation from the chamber of commerce.

"Hello, John. It's good to see you." Kate knew not to take it personally when someone was unhappy with her husband.

"Can I help you with that?" He nodded toward the box.

"That would be lovely. Thank you. My car's just over there." She nodded in the direction of her black Accord. "I'm glad we ran into each other because I have a question for you. When someone loses belongings in a fire, what's the procedure for filing a claim? Do they have to offer proof of some kind that the items were lost?"

John's eyebrows arched in surprise at her question, but as with most people, he enjoyed talking about the work he loved.

"Well, it's best if they can submit receipts. Or if they have a photo or video inventory that gives visual proof of their claim."

"What about family heirlooms? How would you handle the loss of those?"

"Depends on whether they were insured separately. What kind of heirlooms are we talking about? Silver? Jewelry?"

"A painting, specifically."

"Sometimes those are registered, especially when they're bought and sold."

"The one I'm thinking of has always been in private hands."

"Then I guess the agent would have to take his client's word for it. Could there be some sort of record of an appraisal?"

"I don't know about that," Kate said. "I'll have to check." She smiled. "Thanks, John. You've been very helpful."

When they reached her car, Kate unlocked the passenger door, and John gently slid the box onto the seat.

"No problem," he said, then he stopped, worry clouding his expression again. "About that day at the diner with Paul's friend—"

"You don't have to explain anything to me, John. That's

between you and my husband. Besides, I'm sure y'all will work it out, and everything will be fine."

John frowned. "I just wanted to say that I regret going along with Lawton that day. Paul offered us a good opportunity, and we were too stubborn and stuck in our ways to appreciate it." He paused and looked at her intently. "Would you tell Paul that I'm sorry? Pass that message along? We'd like for him to reconsider his resignation."

"I'll tell him, though I think it would mean more coming directly from you." She glanced at her watch. "I'm afraid I have to scoot, but it's good to talk to you."

"Thanks, Kate. Take care."

Kate walked around her car and slid into the driver's seat, wishing she could have stayed longer to chat with John. But he needed to talk with Paul, not her. Paul had never been one to hold a grudge. She hoped the men would be able to work out their differences, because the chamber could certainly benefit from Paul's experience and opinions. She made a mental addition to her prayer list.

Men, Kate thought with a smile. And then she laughed. Perhaps the differences between males and females weren't so big after all.

Chapter Twenty

No matter what time of day or night Kate called Ellen's apartment over the next few days, no one answered. Kate grew more worried with each passing hour. Ellen appeared to have left of her own accord, but Kate had a strong feeling that Oliver must have coerced her in some way.

Oliver's other actions, as reported by Dot and Martha, had definitely raised Kate's suspicions on another count. Why had he been selling off so many items? And were those items connected in any way to the fire?

On Tuesday, the day of her canceled art class, Kate called Livvy to ask her advice. "Now that Ellen's gone, I don't know what to do next."

"*Hmm.*" Livvy was quiet for a moment. "Are you sure you shouldn't do as Ellen asks and let the whole thing go?"

"I want to respect Ellen, but I'm sure Oliver's been pressuring her to say that. I only wish I knew where she was."

"And Dot and Martha say he's been selling stuff all over the area?"

"Yes. I thought he was in Chattanooga looking for one of the paintings, but maybe he was there to sell, not buy."

"Or maybe he's doing both," Livvy said. "Kate, there's a good possibility he didn't really lose anything in that fire."

"That's what I've been thinking. It makes me wonder why Oliver is putting so much effort into selling off these pieces. And why would he lie about their destruction in the first place? A few family heirlooms couldn't bring in that much money. I bought a punch bowl that belonged to Ellen's grandmother for seventy-five dollars."

"Do you want me to check into it?"

"You can do that?"

"The wonders of modern technology. Annual reports of most publicly held companies right at your fingertips. Of course, if his company is privately held, I might need to check tax records. So, I might not have access to everything, but it should be enough to let us know if Oliver has been strapped for cash. And in the meantime . . ."

"I'm going to assume that the last painting wasn't lost in that fire. Do you think if I dropped by the library later, you could print off a list of antique dealers in the area for me?"

"What about Chattanooga?"

"We've already looked there. But maybe it wouldn't hurt to try Nashville. That's where he supposedly attended a board meeting. It's also where Martha and Dot followed him."

"That's a lot of haystacks for one needle," Livvy warned. "How much time do you have left?"

"Not long. I can't imagine the sale of the property will take very much longer to finalize. I'm going to need some help."

"I'd offer, but—"

"No, don't worry. I know just who to call."

Kate thought of Dot and Martha and their keen interest in Ellen's mystery. Since there wasn't much time, she made a plan to divide the list of antique dealers in Nashville and have the pair of them burn up the phone lines.

"I'll let you know what I find out," Livvy said before bidding Kate good-bye and hanging up.

AFTER CALLING MARTHA AND DOT and asking them to meet her at the diner for lunch, Kate headed back to her studio to work on her newest project. She still hadn't figured out how to translate Lela Harrington's style to her stained glass, but she was determined not to give up.

By the time Livvy called to tell Kate she'd found the information on Oliver's finances and had the list of dealers ready for her, Kate wasn't feeling quite as optimistic about either her stained glass work or solving Ellen's mystery. She had continued to place calls to Ellen's apartment at regular intervals, without results, and had begun to contemplate calling the sheriff when Livvy called.

The women spoke briefly, then Kate headed to the library, hoping that Livvy's information would break the current logjam.

"You'll never guess what I found," Livvy said the moment Kate walked through the library doors. "C'mon."

Livvy took her arm and hustled Kate to her office. Once they were alone, she held out a sheaf of papers. "Look. You were right."

"About which part?"

"Oliver has more motivation to commit insurance fraud than you can imagine."

"What did you find?"

Kate slid into a chair across from Livvy's desk, and Livvy settled in across from her. She spread out the papers she'd printed.

"He owes a fortune in back taxes. I found these." She pointed to a sheet covered in numbers. "County tax records. They show delinquencies going back several years."

"So he definitely has motive not only to fake the loss of those heirlooms in that storage-building fire but also to keep Ellen from finding the will." Kate paused. "It seems strange, though, that he would just now sell off the items he claimed to have lost in the fire."

Livvy shrugged. "Perhaps he wanted to wait several years to divert suspicion. Or maybe he's put off paying the taxes as long as he can and needs the money."

Kate brightened. "That fifth painting is out there somewhere. I can feel it."

Livvy frowned. "Be careful not to get carried away, Kate. And remember that if Oliver's that desperate, he could be dangerous."

"I'll remember." She reached over and squeezed Livvy's hand. "Thank you so much."

"What's your next move?"

"I'm meeting Dot and Martha for lunch at the diner. We'll split up the list of antique dealers and get to work calling them to see if we can track down that painting."

"Good luck. I'll send up an extra prayer for guidance."

"I'll take it. Thanks again for the research."

"Always a pleasure doing business with you, Holmes," Livvy teased. "As long as you're in the mystery game, I've got job security."

Kate laughed, then wrinkled her nose. "Neither of us is going to get rich doing this, Watson."

Livvy nodded. "True, but then there's the satisfaction of helping other people. Pretty rewarding in and of itself."

"You better believe it."

They shared a conspiratorial grin, then Kate headed for the diner to meet Martha and Dot.

MARTHA WAS THE ONE who struck gold not two hours after they started making calls. She phoned Kate and could hardly speak because she was so excited.

"Ashley's Antiques and Collectibles in Nashville has a painting that fits the description I gave to the salesperson."

"Did the clerk say what the subject of the painting was?"

Kate had instructed Dot and Martha to ask about anything in the American Primitive style.

"The lady said it was a large Victorian home."

Kate felt a spark of hope ignite. "That could be the big house where Ellen's grandmother lived. The last painting is called *Where My Heart Rests*, so that would fit."

"Do you want the address?" Martha asked.

"Yes, please." She grabbed a pencil and jotted down the information. "You're a treasure, Martha. Dot too."

"We're just tickled to help out," Martha replied.

"I'll keep you posted."

"Are you going right now?"

"As soon as I comb my hair and find my car keys."

"Good luck."

"Thanks, but I think you've already provided that."

Kate called Paul at the church to let him know she was headed to Nashville.

"I think we've found the last painting," she said, brimming with excitement.

"Drive safely," he cautioned her. "I know you're in a hurry, but don't get in too much of a rush."

"I may be late this evening. Do you mind fixing yourself a plate of leftovers?"

"Actually, I'm meeting with the much-maligned Luke Danvers from the community development office. So I'll be late myself."

"You're meeting with him even though you've resigned from the chamber?" Kate smiled.

"I may not be part of that august body anymore, but I still care about this town. If Lawton and his group won't play ball, I'll draft my own team. The governor just announced a new fund for helping smaller towns with economic development. I'm going to talk with Luke to find out how we might take advantage of it."

"I'll be anxious to hear more. See you tonight."

KATE HEEDED PAUL'S WARNING and fought the urge to make her Accord break any speed records on her way to Nashville. At last, though, she found the shop in the Berry Hill District of the city. Once a modest residential neighborhood, the small clapboard houses had been transformed into bead shops, hair salons, and even a do-it-yourself dog wash. Ashley's Antiques and Collectibles inhabited a low-slung weathered building between a doll hospital and a small day-care center.

A bell tinkled above the shop door when Kate entered a few minutes before closing time. The place reminded her of Smith Street Gifts, only it was more dimly lit. She paused in the doorway for a moment so her eyes could adjust to the gloomy interior. Voices carried from the back of the store, but Kate couldn't see the people who were talking. Every inch of space was covered in bric-a-brac and furniture. Paintings lined the walls, and Kate immediately began searching for the one she had come to find.

Her search of the shop quickly proved fruitless, though. Nothing hanging on the walls remotely resembled Lela Harrington's work. Disappointed, Kate decided to find a salesperson and ask about the painting Martha had called about.

She moved toward the back of the store, and as she rounded a large armoire that blocked her view, she saw the salesclerk speaking with two customers. Two very familiar customers, as it turned out.

"Ellen!" Kate hurried forward. Ellen whirled around, as did her cousin Anne. "I'm so glad to see you." Kate's relief was palpable.

"What are you doing here?" Ellen's face was pinched, her tone unwelcoming. "I thought I told you to stay out of this."

Kate stopped, taken aback by Ellen's harsh words. "I came because Martha said they might have the fifth painting—" She broke off when she saw the canvas lying on the sales counter. Kate stepped closer. Sure enough, it was a painting of the big house at Harrington. "You did find it."

"Yes." Anne stepped between Kate and Ellen. "But as Ellen said, this is a private family matter. We both appreciate your help, but perhaps it would be best if you returned to Copper Mill and let us handle this."

"What exactly is it that you need to handle?" Kate asked, every instinct on high alert.

"It's nothing, Kate." Ellen's face was suffused with color. "Please. Just let it go."

"But you have all the pieces to the puzzle now. We can solve it and find the will."

Ellen stepped away from the counter, her face subdued. "It's not worth it, Kate. Not after Oliver's latest threats. I couldn't live with myself if anyone was hurt because of my problem, especially you."

Suddenly Kate understood Ellen's disappearance. "Did Oliver threaten to hurt me? Oh, Ellen, no one's going to do anything to harm me. Besides, we're almost done now that you and Anne have found this painting." Kate wasn't beyond imploring the pair to follow the clues until they found what they were looking for. "You don't really want to quit now, do you? Otherwise you wouldn't have come looking for this last painting like I did. Please, Ellen, I would hate to abandon the search for your grandfather's will when we're so close to solving the mystery."

Anne cleared her throat. "For what it's worth, Ellen, I think she's right." Then she turned to Kate. "Ellen was very concerned about Oliver's threats toward you, Kate. But perhaps we're overestimating his strength and under-estimating your savvy." She paused for a moment, then went on. "Like Ellen, I tired of this lifelong family feud. I thought I could cut myself off from it, but when she showed up on my doorstep today, I realized I've been wrong about where my obligations lie." She looked at Ellen. "I know we said we were only looking for this paint-ing so that Oliver couldn't get his hands on it, but let's solve this mystery once and for all. If we can't and Oliver gets his way, then so be it. But we should at least try—"

"All right, all right." Ellen held up a hand, a smile play-ing at the corners of her mouth. "I know when I'm out-numbered." She reached over and gave Kate a quick hug. "I don't know what I've done to deserve your friendship, but I'll try to keep on doing it, whatever it is. Thanks for not giving up on me, Kate."

Kate grinned. "Like I told you before, when I'm puz-zling out a mystery, I'm like a dog with a bone. I just can't stop until I've followed the clues all the way to the end."

"Then let's get going. We have all five paintings now, so let's go study them." Ellen reached for the painting on the counter, thanked the saleswoman, who had witnessed the whole conversation with a half smile on her face, and then nodded at Anne.

"You're welcome to come back with us to Pine Ridge," Ellen said. "If you're so inclined."

Anne shook her head. "Much as I'd like to, I have to leave town in the morning. My husband's flying to Europe on business, and I'm accompanying him."

"Then I guess it's just the two of us," Ellen said to Kate. "Shall we?"

The three women made their way out of the shop. Ellen slid the painting into the backseat of her compact.

"I'll follow you," Kate said. "That way I can keep an eye on you in case you try to escape," she teased.

Ellen laughed, but then her expression sobered. "I'm sorry about disappearing on you, but I was afraid of putting you in danger. You were right. It was Oliver. He came back to my apartment, threatening me with legal action and everything else he could think of. Said I had to quit interfering in his business matters. And then when he threatened you . . ." She gave a rueful laugh. "I guess I panicked. It's all been so stressful, with my husband's death, the move to Pine Ridge, and now all of this craziness about the will."

"It's almost over," Kate reassured her. "With all the paintings, we should be able to solve the mystery now."

Kate called home and left a message on the answering machine so Paul would know of her change in plans. The drive from Nashville to Pine Ridge gave her plenty of time to think. She knew they shouldn't underestimate Oliver, especially since he'd been resorting to intimidation and scare tactics. But she also didn't think they should allow him to dictate their decisions.

Once they were safely ensconced in Ellen's apartment

with the paintings, Kate knew it was time to tell her what Livvy had uncovered about Oliver's finances.

"Back taxes? I'm surprised. Oliver was always such a hospital corners kind of guy. So meticulous about everything."

"Maybe he got so caught up in appearances that he couldn't admit when his business started to fail."

"It sounds like he really does need the money from Carol's share of the property."

"Evidently."

Ellen shook her head. "Just when you think it can't get any worse. I feel sorry for Carol."

"Sorry enough to abandon the search?"

"No. Even if it distresses Carol, I have to try and save High Hoot Ridge."

"And yourself too."

Ellen waved a hand. "You know, I'm not even that concerned about my own finances anymore. All of this has made me rethink what I want out of the rest of my life." She gazed around the room, then looked at Kate. "I thought I'd come home just to mark time until . . . well, until I died. Like Trevor."

"And now?"

She smiled. "Well, now I realize I have quite a bit of living left to do."

"Well," Kate said, "since we're not giving up, how about we line up these canvases and see what we can figure out?"

Ellen nodded enthusiastically and helped Kate spread

the paintings across one side of the small living room, propping them against whatever was handy. But try as they might, they couldn't see the clue that Ellen's grandmother had meant for her to find.

"I'm sorry, Kate," Ellen said after a half hour of intense study, "but I just can't make heads or tails of it." Ellen sank onto the sofa. "What on earth could my grandmother have meant to communicate in these paintings?"

"I'm sure there's something we've overlooked."

"They're just random scenes from Harrington. We've gone over them with a fine-tooth comb."

"From everything you've said, your grandmother wasn't the kind of person to lead you on a fruitless treasure hunt. And she said it's something only you could see."

"I've applied every theory, every kind of art criticism I can think of. But there are no stylistic differences. The color palette is consistent. No classical allusions or secret signs of any kind. They're just paintings of Harrington."

"Okay, you have the big house, the church, the company store and the post office, the pristine scene of High Hoot Ridge, and the ironworks. Maybe they're a map since they depict actual places."

"But the pristine scene of the ridge and the ironworks are the same place. Why would she paint it twice? And why would she have two buildings in one painting but not in the others?" Ellen asked, pointing toward the picture of the company store and the post office.

"Okay, so they're not meant to be a map. Maybe it's a code of some kind, like the first letter of each location."

Ellen looked intrigued. "Maybe. *H* for High Hoot Ridge. *I* for the ironworks. *B* for the big house. But do you use *C* for church or *S* for schoolhouse? And what about the company store and the post office? Which letter would you use for that painting?"

Kate sighed. "You're right. That doesn't make any sense. Besides, I would think that whatever your grandmother intended, it would have something to do with the pictures themselves. Maybe they tell some kind of story?"

Both women scrutinized the paintings once more, but after a few minutes, they exchanged a look of defeat.

"Maybe we should sleep on it," Kate suggested. "It's been a long day, and you've had enough stress to last you for a while."

"Would you mind coming back in the morning?" Ellen asked. "Surely between the two of us—"

"Wait a minute." Kate stopped Ellen in midsentence. "I have an idea."

"I'm definitely open to new ideas."

"I think I might know someone who can help us. But I need you to let me borrow the paintings."

"Of course. But who?"

Kate chuckled. "Someone who probably knows more about all these places"—she gestured toward the paintings—"than anyone else still living."

"And that would be?"

"His name is Joshua Parsons, and he's a lifelong resident of Copper Mill. He worked in the copper mines when he was young, but he also knows a lot about Harrington and the ironworks," Kate said. "I'll take the paintings to him first thing in the morning, and then I'll give you a call."

"Promise?"

"As long as you stay put," Kate said, giving Ellen a knowing look for emphasis. "If you hear from Oliver again, hold your ground. Better yet, hang up on him. Or shut the door in his face."

"Kate, you have to take him seriously. We're just learning how desperate he really is."

"I promise to be careful. Hopefully Oliver is home recovering from last week's board of directors meeting."

Ellen wrapped four of the paintings in brown wrapping paper and handed Kate one of the blown-up photographs of Oliver's painting. Kate would take photos of all the paintings when she got home. Then she helped Kate carry them out to her car.

"Give me a call tomorrow, okay?" Ellen said.

Kate nodded. "With any luck, I'll have some better news for you."

As Kate drove off, she could see Ellen standing on the sidewalk waving good-bye. Kate felt a twinge of sadness, knowing that whatever happened with the will, Ellen would still have a number of issues left to resolve. She would need more time to mourn the loss of her husband, but at least she had mended fences with her cousin Anne. And they seemed to have most of the information they needed to resolve the ownership of High Hoot Ridge once and for all. Maybe things were looking up for Ellen after all.

Chapter Twenty-One

The next morning, Kate found it difficult to juggle her handbag, a fudge pie, and the photos she'd made of all the paintings, but she finally managed to wrangle all three items plus herself to Joshua Parsons' front door. Fortunately, he opened the door before Kate was forced to find a way to knock.

"Hello there." Old Man Parsons looked her over and then seemed to relax when he spotted the pie. "I've been looking forward to this."

Kate wasn't quite sure whether he meant he was anticipating her visit or the pie she brought with her. Probably the latter, she decided with a smile.

"I'm glad to hear that," Kate said. "It's always nice to be the cause of anticipation rather than dread."

Parsons laughed in his thin, reedy voice and waved her inside. "Here. Let me take that."

Kate thought he was reaching for the packet of photos, but he relieved her of the pie instead. Kate bit her lip to keep from chuckling. She followed him into the house and set her handbag on a nearby chair. Parsons had already disappeared into the kitchen.

"Didn't happen to bring any coffee, did you?" he called.

Kate followed his voice and found him standing at the counter, cutting into the pie.

"Of course." Kate set the thermos she'd retrieved from her handbag on the counter.

"This is wonderful. My wife, Alma, used to make the best fudge pie in Copper Mill, and it tasted best with a hot cup of coffee."

"You may find mine a poor substitute," Kate warned him.

He shook his head. "Kate, when you're an old man like me, living all alone, you learn to enjoy your blessings, not compare them."

Kate nodded at his words of wisdom. "Well said, Mr. Parsons."

He picked up a plate that held an enormous slice of pie and offered it to her. "Will you join me?"

Kate shook her head. "I'd better not. But I'll sit with you while you eat." Kate poured him a cup of coffee— black, of course—and set it next to his plate.

"So, what brings you back to see an old man like me? Besides the fact that you promised me another pie."

Kate wondered if her agenda was written on her face. "I thought I'd pick your brain again, if you didn't mind."

"You're welcome to what's left of it, young lady."

"Well, you're the only person I know of who remembers the town of Harrington and the ironworks. I thought you might be able to help me."

"I'm glad to do what I can."

"If you'd take a look at photos of some paintings," she said, "I'd be grateful. They form a puzzle of sorts, but I can't seem to solve it."

"Now I'm intrigued," he said between bites of pie.

Five minutes later, he had finished his pie and Kate had lined up the photos on Old Man Parsons' coffee table in the living room. They sat side by side on his well-worn sofa.

"These are by Lela Harrington, that woman in the newspaper article I showed you last time you were here," Joshua said the moment he saw them.

"Yes. She painted them."

Joshua rubbed his chin and studied each picture one by one while Kate held her breath. If only he could see in the paintings whatever she and Ellen were missing.

Finally, after several minutes, he shook his head. "They're nice enough, but I don't see any hidden messages in them."

"Are they accurate, as far as you remember? In terms of the buildings and settings, I mean. Is there anything off kilter or that doesn't seem right?" Kate asked, hoping against hope.

Again, Joshua shook his head. "I expect they're as accurate as anything could be in that kind of thing." He frowned. "Looks like a kindergartner painted them. Never did understand this modern stuff."

Kate decided there was no need to point out that the American Primitive style had long since passed its prime, and the art world had moved on.

"Well, I appreciate your taking time to look at them. It was worth a try."

"If there's a puzzle there, well, I certainly don't—" He stopped and then crossed his arms over his bony chest, still staring at the paintings. "Wait a minute." He leaned forward.

Kate watched as Joshua began to move them around, pulling one from the end to the middle and switching two others. When he was done, he leaned back and surveyed all of them once more.

"What is it?" Kate asked, moving to stand beside him. She still couldn't see whatever it was that he evidently saw.

"Well, at first I thought they were just different scenes from Harrington. But I couldn't figure out why she'd paint High Hoot Ridge when everything else was from a later time period."

"And?" Kate's heart raced.

"I think I've figured out your mystery," Joshua said with a sly grin. "If I tell you the answer, will you come back soon with another pie?"

Kate had to laugh. "Mr. Parsons, if you've solved this puzzle, I'll make you any pie of your choice, with a cherry on top."

Her answer must have satisfied him, because right then and there in Old Man Parsons' living room, Kate discovered the secret of the paintings and the location of the missing will.

Chapter Twenty-Two

Kate pulled her car into the garage and let out a sigh of relief. Finally the mystery was solved. Yet she also knew that her role in the matter was far from over. Finding the will would set a whole new series of problems into motion. Oliver would be furious, and Kate worried about what he might do. They needed a way to minimize any damage he might try to cause.

She was worried about Carol too, who would always be at risk from Oliver's wrath. Then there was Ellen's dream of restoring Harrington. Was there any hope of making it come true? Kate thought so, but she'd have to talk to Paul first. And finally, but least pressing, was the fact that she was way behind on her class project. Surely her professor would cut her some slack, she thought to herself with a chuckle.

The first thing she had to do, though, was to call Ellen and tell her the good news.

"I've been sitting by the phone all morning," Ellen said. "What did you find out?"

"I know where the will is," Kate said, and Ellen shrieked. Kate had to pull the phone away from her ear.

"I can't believe it. Mr. Parsons solved the mystery?"

"He sure did," Kate said. "He remembers a great deal about Harrington, so he was able to put two and two together."

"How? What did we miss?"

"Well, the one thing we forgot to consider was the chronological order of the paintings. The sequence in which the places featured in the paintings were developed."

Kate could hear Ellen groan.

"Of course," Ellen said. "It's so simple. I should have seen that."

"I didn't catch it either."

"But you didn't grow up on my grandmother's stories of the founding of the town. I sat next to her for hours, listening to her tell me about it."

"But how do you know where the will is? There's still no X to mark the spot."

"I'll show you tomorrow."

"Tomorrow?" Ellen exhaled loudly. "I can't wait that long."

"I'm afraid you'll have to. I've been doing some thinking, and it seems to me that we have more problems than simply finding the will."

"Such as?"

"Such as how to handle Oliver, and whether you can reconcile with Carol. And the future of your past, so to speak."

"What do you mean?"

"I'll pick you up in the morning at ten o'clock. Dress comfortably."

"Kate! You can't do this to me."

"You're going to have to trust me on this one," Kate advised her. "I promise it will be worth it."

Ellen sighed. "All right. But only because I'd never have found the will without you."

"I hope that by the time I'm through, you'll have a lot more than just a piece of paper," Kate said. "Now, I've got to run, or I'll never be ready by tomorrow."

"I'll be waiting outside. Don't be afraid to come early," Ellen said with a sigh, but she also sounded happier than Kate had ever heard her.

"Tomorrow. Get a good night's sleep tonight, okay?"

"Sleep? Hah."

Kate wondered whether she'd be able to sleep herself, but not because of anxiety. No, any lack of shut-eye would be because she had a great deal of work to do before then to put her plan in motion. And the first step was to talk with Paul. She was going to need his help.

FORTUNATELY FOR KATE, Paul didn't have a lunch appointment that day, so he was more than happy to come home for a bowl of soup and a grilled cheese sandwich. She waited until they'd eaten to broach the subject.

"We've solved Ellen's mystery, thanks to Joshua Parsons."

Paul wiped his mouth with his napkin and sat back in

his chair at the kitchen table. "That's good news. But you don't look as relieved as I would have thought."

"Well, finding the will is going to present a whole new set of problems. Ones I need your help resolving."

"You know I'm happy to do whatever I can."

"Do you remember when I told you about Ellen's dream of bringing Harrington back to life?"

Paul nodded. "Sure."

"I want to do more than just solve the mystery. I want to help her achieve her dream."

"That's a pretty tall order, Kate."

"Hear me out first. Once Ellen has the will in her possession, she'll have as much claim to that property as Oliver Coats. So she can stop the sale to the paper company."

"That's what you've been hoping for all along, right?"

"Yes, but it's not enough. She needs leverage to get Oliver to agree to sell the land—at least most of it—to the state as a wildlife preserve. She and Carol will keep the old town and the ironworks."

"So what kind of leverage does she need?"

"Nothing unsavory. Just something to motivate him." She briefly explained what Livvy had uncovered about Oliver's finances. "I was hoping you might have some ideas about how to get him to agree to Ellen's plans."

"Do you know for sure whether he's committed fraud?"

"No. But I suppose I could go to the sheriff with what I know. He'd at least look into it." She paused. "But if I do that, Oliver will fight Ellen tooth and nail."

"He sounds like a man who always does what's in his own best interests," Paul said. "Could you convince him that Ellen's plan would serve him better?"

"Maybe." Kate stared out the window as she considered Paul's question. "If his business is failing, you'd think he'd want to improve the local economy. And reviving Harrington as a tourist attraction would certainly help."

Paul snapped his fingers. "Kate, you're a genius."

She beamed at him. "I was hoping you'd say that."

He raised his eyebrows in surprise. "You already know what I'm going to suggest?"

"I think so. It's the conclusion I was hoping you'd reach."

"It could all come together, couldn't it?" Paul asked with enthusiasm. "A way to preserve the past and help provide for the future. But how do we get everyone on the same page?"

"I have a few thoughts about that," Kate said. "If you don't have to head straight back to the church."

Paul crossed his arms and smiled. "I'm all ears."

"Well, I need you to round up the chamber of commerce. And the man you met with last night from the state community development office."

"Round them up when?"

"Tomorrow at lunchtime."

"And what do I tell them?"

"You can tell the state official the whole truth. As for Lawton and the other fellows, just say they're invited to a special luncheon. I'll arrange to have Ellen there."

"And Oliver?"

"I don't think he needs to be in on the plans until they're firm," Kate said. "I'd just as soon leave him out of it for now. We'll be able to prove Ellen's claim to the property, so we won't be trespassing."

"You really think we can pull this off?"

"As long as I'm right about the location of the will."

Paul reached over and squeezed her hand. "Have I said recently how amazing you are?"

"Well, wait and see what happens tomorrow. Then we'll see if *amazing* is the right word."

"I don't doubt it will be." He leaned over to brush a kiss on her lips. "Now, if you'll excuse me, I have a few phone calls to make to set up a very important meeting tomorrow."

"I have one or two things to accomplish myself." Kate gave him a wink, then picked up their plates and carried them to the sink. "And I'll need you a little later on for a special assignment."

"Once you find the will, maybe things will be quiet for a change," Paul teased.

"And maybe I finally can get some work done on my class project."

"That was what got you into this quagmire in the first place, wasn't it?" Paul teased. "Your desire for more education?"

Kate reached for the dishtowel and pretended to swat at him. "Now enough of that, Paul Hanlon. You've got work to do. Shoo."

Paul chuckled as he retreated through the kitchen entryway. Then he called out "Love you!" just before Kate heard the front door close behind him. She knew he would do his best to make sure his share of the arrangements were in place for the following day.

She wiped her hands on the dishtowel, then reached for the phone. She punched in a number that had become very familiar over the past few weeks.

"Martha? It's Kate. I don't know if you're busy tomorrow, but I sure could use your help."

Martha, of course, couldn't be more delighted at the request and volunteered to enlist Dot's help as well. Ten minutes later, the wheels were in motion, and Kate was more optimistic than ever that Ellen's dream of restoring Harrington would come true.

Chapter Twenty-Three

The next morning, Kate, Ellen, Martha, and Dot stuffed every nook and cranny of Kate's trunk with supplies, then piled into her car and headed for High Hoot Ridge. Kate had wanted them to get an early start so that they'd have enough time to prepare for their lunch guests.

"You're sure you don't want to tell us what you've got up your sleeve?" Ellen asked as Kate drove up the winding dirt road. "Other than feeding an army?"

"It's a surprise," Kate said. "Let's just say we're having an impromptu party." She could see Martha and Dot beaming with anticipation in the backseat.

Ellen shook her head, but the hint of a smile played around her lips. "For a minister's wife, you're pretty sneaky."

"I try," Kate said.

Golden fall sunshine dappled the trees, the leaves turning orange and yellow. Kate couldn't have asked for a more beautiful day to put her plan into action.

"Here we are." This time, she followed the rutted remains of the road around the curve until she came to a stop in front of the big house.

"I've never been up here," Martha said, climbing out of the car, "but my mother used to talk about it."

After they unloaded the supplies from the car, Ellen showed Dot and Martha around the little town. Meanwhile Kate set up a makeshift table on the porch of the big house, using a couple of sawhorses and a length of plywood, then she covered it with a piece of oilcloth. By the time the ladies returned, she was setting out plates of sandwiches and side items.

"It looks delicious," Ellen said. "How can I help?"

"There's a box over there," Kate said, nodding toward the porch steps. "But be careful. It has breakables."

Ellen carried the box onto the porch and began to open it. Kate set out the napkins and flatware as she watched Ellen out of the corner of her eye.

"My grandmother's punch bowl!" Ellen drew the object from the box and lovingly caressed the edges of the cut glass. "I can't believe it. Where did you find it?" She looked at Kate in disbelief.

"Fortunately I was in Smith Street Gifts not too long after Oliver had been there doing business." Kate poured punch into the bowl. "He must have gotten his hands on it somewhere along the way. I knew you'd want to have it."

"Thank you." She stopped and looked at Kate across the table. "I know I seem to be saying that with great regularity, but I am truly grateful."

"Oh, just wait," Kate teased. "You haven't seen anything yet."

All of Ellen's pleas, though, couldn't entice Kate to say anymore. With all four women working away, they had the luncheon ready to serve in no time.

"I hope there are a lot of people coming," Dot said, dubiously eyeing the bounty spread across the table.

"Actually, we're going to have quite a few guests," Kate said. "They should be here any moment."

As if on cue, she heard the familiar sound of Paul's truck approaching. Kate walked over to the top of the porch steps and saw two cars following Paul. The first she recognized as Lawton Briddle's Buick. The second was a plain white sedan with the state emblem emblazoned on the side.

"Who's that?" Ellen came to stand beside Kate.

"Our party guests," Kate answered cryptically. She descended the steps and walked to Paul's truck. Peering into the bed, she saw the paintings, wrapped in protective coverings, stowed in the back.

"We're here." Paul announced the obvious as he came around the back of the truck to greet her. "Where do you want these?"

"Up on the porch, please. We'll line them up under the windows."

"Yes, ma'am." Paul winked at her and set about unloading the paintings.

Kate left him to his task and went to greet the mayor, who had brought Fred Cowan and John Sharpe with him.

Clifton was taking care of Ida Mae and hadn't been able to make it. All three men looked dubious as they took in their surroundings.

"Good day, Mrs. Hanlon," Lawton said, tipping his hat to her. "I'm not sure what your husband meant by dragging us up here, but—"

"He did it at my request, Mayor. I had something I wanted y'all to see."

Another man, whom Kate had never met, joined the group.

"I'm Luke Danvers," he said, offering his hand to Kate. "Your husband has told me a lot about you."

"Thank you for coming, Mr. Danvers. We have lunch ready up there on the porch."

At the mention of food, all the men looked up with interest.

"Follow me, and we'll get you fed," Kate said. "The ladies will be happy to serve you."

Paul had displayed the paintings, and Kate asked him to say a blessing over the meal. Moments later, the men were huddled around the makeshift buffet, plates in hand, while the women poured tea and punch and generally played hostess.

"What's going on?" Ellen whispered to Kate as she slid deviled eggs onto Lawton Briddle's plate. "Why are these men here?"

"You'll see." Kate shot her a mysterious smile.

By the time the ladies had filled their plates and found a place to eat, the men were happily munching away. Paul was encouraging Luke Danvers to tell the group about the new rural development fund the governor had initiated, and for once, Lawton and his cronies were listening instead of talking. Kate couldn't help but wonder whether Paul's frustrated departure from the chamber had been just what the men needed to wake up.

Her plan was going splendidly, Kate thought. She had just taken a bite of her sandwich when she heard the sound of another car coming up the ridge.

"Who's that?" Martha asked.

A large black Lincoln Continental appeared through the trees. It growled ominously as it pulled to a stop behind Paul's pickup truck.

Ellen stepped to the porch rail, a horrified expression on her face.

"It's Oliver," she said, a tremor in her voice.

Kate had planned some surprises for the day, but Oliver's sudden appearance wasn't one of them.

"How did he know we were up here?" she asked Ellen.

The other woman shook her head. "I have no idea. Maybe he followed us."

Oliver was out of his car now, striding across the ground toward the big house. Kate's stomach knotted as he mounted the porch steps with barely concealed hostility.

"You are all trespassing," he said, his cheeks red and his eyes blazing. "I'm ordering you to leave right now."

Lawton Briddle set his plate down, rose from his seat, and walked over to Oliver. Paul followed him.

"What's going on here, Oliver?" The mayor frowned. "What's got you so riled?"

"You are trespassing on private property."

Paul shrugged his shoulders. "Just having a little picnic and talking with Mr. Danvers here about how the state might be able to help us with some business development." He shot a pointed look at Oliver. "Since you're here, I'd think you'd be interested in being a part of that conversation."

Oliver opened his mouth to protest, but Paul continued. "Besides, I can't see why you'd begrudge your wife's cousin Ellen a little time up here. It's their family's home place, isn't it?"

Kate stepped forward. "I was just about to show everyone something very interesting I found, Oliver. Perhaps you'd care to join us?"

She felt a small measure of satisfaction when his eyebrows shot up in alarm. After his actions toward Ellen, Kate had little sympathy for the man. She did, however, feel some compassion. Desperate men took desperate measures. But she hoped to show him that he didn't have to feel—or be—desperate anymore.

"I can't imagine you have anything that important to show anyone," he growled, "but I'm not leaving until you do."

"Fine." Kate turned to the others who were scattered around the porch, some perched against the railing, others standing near the table with their plates in hand.

"If everyone is about finished, I have a bit of an art show to share with you."

Kate looked at Ellen, who was glowing with anticipation. This was the moment she'd been waiting for all these weeks.

"Ellen Carruthers and I have managed to collect several of her grandmother Lela Harrington's paintings. As you can see"—Kate waved a hand toward the canvases lined up along the front of the house—"they all depict scenes from this place. But what you may not know," she said, nodding toward Luke Danvers and the men from the chamber of commerce, "is that these paintings are also clues to a hidden will."

"This is all bunk—" Oliver protested, then fell silent.

Kate turned just in time to see the threatening look the mayor was giving Oliver.

"Please let my wife continue," Paul said politely but firmly.

Kate stepped toward the paintings, which Paul had placed in random order. One by one, with her husband's assistance, she began to move the paintings around until they were in their proper order. First came the landscape of High Hoot Ridge. Then the photograph of the ironworks. That was followed by the depiction of the company store and the post office. Fourth was the combination church and school building. And last came the painting of the big house where they were all standing.

"Lela Harrington told her granddaughter in a private letter that these paintings would lead to the missing will. But what Ellen didn't know was how to decode them. With the help of a wonderful source in Copper Mill, Joshua Parsons, we have learned that the clue lies in the chronological order of the landmarks the paintings portray."

Kate saw Ellen's eyes darken with understanding. They shared a knowing smile. "Do you want to take it from here?" Kate asked Ellen.

"Oh yes." She moved to stand beside Kate. "Of course. It makes complete sense now. It was there all along, wasn't it?"

Paul chuckled. "Well, I wish you ladies would explain it to me, because I still don't understand."

"My grandmother always used to tell me that I would find something that was lost in the last place I looked," Ellen said.

"Didn't everyone's grandmother say that?" Martha asked, confusion lining her face.

"I'm sure they did. But my grandmother meant it specifically. About my grandfather's second will—"

"There's no such thing," Oliver said, interrupting. "I don't know why you won't accept that." But he didn't sound very convinced.

"Yes, there is a will. And thanks to Kate here, I know where it is." She gestured toward the final painting of the big house. "This home was the last building to be completed in Harrington. My grandmother's paintings are supposed to remind me of the development of the ironworks and the town, all leading to this place, her home."

"That doesn't narrow it down quite as much as you might hope," Paul said.

"Actually," Kate replied, "it does. Once Mr. Parsons showed me where to look, I had no trouble finding this." She pointed toward the canvas. "If you come closer, you can see a small glass bowl—most likely a Fostoria bowl—of apples right here on the porch. I expect the will is right underneath the floorboards there. That's the only thing all the paintings have in common, you see. Somewhere in each of them, you can find apples."

Oliver bristled. "That's the most foolish thing I've ever heard. You're not ripping up this porch on such flimsy evidence."

"Oh, we don't have to rip it up," Kate said. She crossed to where her boxes of supplies were stacked against the far railing. "Paul and I came up here late yesterday afternoon with a crowbar and realized the boards didn't even need to be pried up. They were already loose." She pointed toward a spot just beneath Oliver's feet. "In fact, it was right there, where you're standing, Mr. Coats."

Kate reached into one of the cardboard boxes and withdrew a rusted lockbox. She took the box over to Ellen and placed it in her hands. "For you," she said.

"Wait. If you found that here, it's my property," Oliver said, moving forward. But Fred and John quickly stepped into his path, blocking his way.

"Let her open it," Lawton Briddle said. He drew a penknife from his pocket and offered it to Ellen. "You might need this."

Ellen set the box on the table and, with trembling hands, used the knife to pry open the lid. After several moments of struggle, it popped free. Kate stepped forward, hoping against hope that her plan wasn't going to go awry now that they'd reached the critical moment. She hadn't thought it right to open the box herself. Whatever was in it would be just as much a surprise to her as it would be to everyone else.

Ellen reached into the lockbox and drew out a plastic bag. It had been sealed with a twist tie. Inside was a yellowed piece of paper that had been folded in half.

"My hands are shaking too badly," Ellen said and thrust the bag into Kate's hands. "You open it."

Kate wasn't sure her own nerves were much better, but she did as instructed. Carefully, she drew out the sheet of paper and unfolded it.

Kate recognized the handwriting instantly. It was the same writing she'd seen when Oliver had thrust the first will at her that day in his study. Ellen looked over Kate's shoulder at the paper, and tears started pouring down her cheeks.

"Read it," Paul said, and Kate cleared her throat.

"All right. It says,

I, Alexander Harrington, being of sound mind and body, do bequeath all of my worldly possessions, including my interest in the land on High Hoot Ridge, to my granddaughter, Ellen Harrington. This is my last will and testament and should take the place of any others so attested to by me.

"It's signed in his hand," Kate said. "Oliver Coats showed me a copy of Alexander Harrington's first will, and the handwriting is exactly the same. It's dated after the first one."

"That can't be real." Oliver thrust an accusing finger at Kate. "You forged it. Pretended to find it here. It's all lies."

Paul stepped forward. "I was with my wife yesterday when she found the box."

"I'm just saying—" Oliver began, then stopped. His face fell and his shoulders slumped, as if all the air had been knocked out of him. He sank against the porch rail and put his head in his hands. "This can't be happening. This sale has to go through or I'm ruined."

"Perhaps there are some other options," Kate said to him with as much kindness as she could muster. "Ellen has some ideas about how to use the land. And now she has a share in those decisions."

Oliver looked up, his bleak gaze pinned on Ellen. "Why did you have to come back?"

Ellen returned his look, long and hard. "Because family matters, Oliver. History matters. I needed to learn that. Maybe you do too."

"Money is what matters," he snapped back, his animosity returning. "You're naive to think otherwise."

Ellen was clearly out of patience with the man. "You can have some money, Oliver, or none at all," she said, holding her ground. "I won't agree to any sale unless it's to the state for a wildlife preserve. And the family retains the town site and the ironworks."

"For what possible reason would you want to hold on to these run-down old buildings?"

Kate nodded at Ellen. "Why don't you tell him and these other fine gentlemen as well?" She grinned. "In fact, why don't you give them the same tour that you gave Martha and Dot? Might help them see the possibilities."

Ellen's eyes shone with joy, the first time Kate could recall seeing her that way.

"That's a wonderful idea," Ellen said. "If everyone would come with me, I'd like to show you my heritage and explain why I think it would be suitable for some serious investment as a profitable tourist destination."

Luke Danvers looked very interested, and even Lawton Briddle was nodding as Ellen spoke.

"Please, go on," Kate said. "The ladies and I will clean up."

With nods and murmurs of assent, all the men except Paul followed Ellen down the steps. Kate wanted to jump in the air and let out a hoot in victory. Instead, she settled for energetically humming a favorite hymn while she gathered paper plates and began to pack away the luncheon leftovers.

Thank you, Lord, she prayed, her heart overflowing with gratitude. *You never cease to amaze me. Your fingerprints are all over this, and I know you can even bring Oliver Coats around.*

AS IT TURNED OUT, Oliver went on the town tour with the others, then lingered after Luke Danvers said good-bye, promising to be in touch with the chamber about government funding. Oliver was still there when Lawton, Fred, and John drove off down the ridge. And even when Martha and Dot went to supervise Paul as he loaded the boxes into Kate's car, Oliver stayed put on the porch. He looked like a sullen schoolboy, but at least his anger seemed spent.

"I don't have to agree to this, you know," he said to Kate and Ellen once Paul was out of earshot. "I may not get my way, but you won't get yours either."

"I'm not sure you're in much of a position to object," Kate pointed out. "Not after what you've done. Threatening Ellen and me. Trying to come between her and her cousins. Lying. You told me that the last painting was destroyed in the fire, but it clearly wasn't."

Oliver's face sank as if he'd finally been drained of his last ounce of energy. "I'll go under because of your interference."

"No, if your company fails, it will be because of your decisions, not mine," Ellen said.

Kate was proud of Ellen for standing her ground so well against Oliver.

"If the state's willing to provide some money to rebuild Harrington," Ellen went on, "there will be a lot of business opportunities. Maybe your company could put in a bid to work on the railroad line that will be needed. Other companies would bid on the project as well, but you'd have a fair chance, just like everyone else. Plus, you'd have a unique knowledge of the area that other companies might not have."

Oliver looked interested but dubious. "Perhaps."

"In any case," Ellen said, "we're going to have to work together. As a family. And I want Carol included in the process. As well as Anne." She paused. "Now that I have family ties again, I'm not going to relinquish them quite so easily."

If nothing else, Oliver Coats was a man who knew when he'd been bested.

"All right. You win." He pulled himself up to his full height. "I'll be in touch."

"As will I."

The two women watched him pound down the porch steps and stride toward his car.

"I'm so proud of you," Kate said, giving Ellen a hug. "You've come a long way in a short time."

"Thanks to you." Ellen returned her hug, then looked at Kate. "Do you think we can really pull this off? Turn Harrington into a winning proposition?"

Kate smiled. "With hard work and a lot of prayer, I think it will be splendid."

"I do too."

Kate's gaze followed Ellen's out over the ridge and along the treetops. Kate had found during her time in Copper Mill that solving mysteries were about so much more than finding the answers. Her efforts had more to do with rebuilding relationships than ferreting out hidden truths. And maybe that was fitting, given that the human heart was often the biggest mystery of all.

Epilogue

Six weeks later

"Y ou can see from this slide," Kate said, pausing to click her laptop mouse so that the next picture showed on the screen, "that the artist knew her subject intimately."

Lela Harrington's painting of the big house drew some murmurs of appreciation from Kate's young classmates. She let them study the work for several long moments before she continued.

"As I said at the beginning, her work in this series of paintings details the development of the ironworks and the company town owned by her husband's family."

Kate's presentation was going far better than she'd dared hope. Despite the distraction of searching for the missing will, she'd learned an enormous amount in Ellen's class.

"As with other painters like van Gogh or Monet, you can see the artist's love for her setting in the telling details, such as the use of color or the placement of the figures in the painting. In this work"—she clicked again to zoom in on a smaller portion of the painting—"you can peek into one of the windows in the artist's home."

Through a second-story window, Lela had shown softly billowing curtains and a glimpse of a young girl sound asleep in her bed. Kate had no doubt that the girl was meant to be a young Ellen.

"And here is an example of the artist's influence on my own work."

Kate hadn't been sure whether to include the picture of her latest piece of stained glass, but Ellen had insisted. After much experimentation, Kate had found a way to incorporate the influence of the American Primitive style into her own work. The framed piece, a foot and a half across and two feet high, might not have the childlike detail of a painting, but Kate had chosen the same bold colors Ellen's grandmother had used. The glass depicted the little town of Harrington with a glimpse of the iron-works in the distance.

Finished with her presentation, Kate clicked so that the picture faded to black. Ellen flipped on the overhead lights, and the students blinked.

"Thank you, Kate. That was nicely done." Ellen beamed her approval, and Kate knew it was for much more than her final project.

After class, she and Ellen walked out of the building together for the last time.

"How's the development in Harrington coming along?" Kate asked.

Ellen made a noncommittal noise. "Well, Oliver's

being difficult, of course. But Carol's finally finding the gumption to stand up to him from time to time. It is her family's land, after all."

"And Anne?"

"She says she'll go with whatever I want."

"So you'll get there eventually," Kate said.

"Yes, we will."

"Good. And I know I'm prying, but I have to ask. Paul said Bill called and asked for your phone number."

Ellen blushed, which was all the answer Kate needed.

"I'm going to visit him in San Antonio over Christmas break," Ellen said, then she laughed. "I feel like a school-girl again, much to my chagrin."

"Good." Kate stopped and turned to her newfound friend. "Just please don't let him take you away from here. You've got a lot of work to do. And friends who would miss you."

"Thanks to you." Ellen gave her a quick hug. "You helped me reclaim my past, and now I have a future."

"As do a lot more people around here."

Paul had mentioned just that morning that Mike Rowland had been hired as a construction worker on the Harrington project. Luke Danvers had become an enthu-siastic supporter of the idea. Kate had no idea if Oliver's company would win the contract to construct the neces-sary railroad, but she hoped he would. She wanted him to have a second chance.

"What will you do with all your free time now?" Ellen teased.

"Oh, I'm sure I'll keep myself occupied."

Paul had rejoined the chamber of commerce after some cajoling on the part of Lawton Briddle, and Kate had agreed to coordinate the Christmas Craft Extravaganza. She had a feeling that would keep her busy through the end of the year, or at least until a new mystery came along.

"Well, you need to keep working on your stained glass," Ellen said. "I'm sure we'll want to carry your work in the company store once the town is up and running."

Kate nodded. "I know of several local craftspeople who would be eager to talk to you about selling their work as well."

Ellen smiled. "You know, I thought solving this mystery was just about me, but as it turns out, it was really about the future of our little part of the world in Harrington County." Her expression sobered a little. "We're all connected, aren't we? Even when we don't realize it."

Kate thought of the little community of Copper Mill and the surrounding towns, of all the people she'd come to know and love. As difficult as it had been to leave behind the amenities of a big city like San Antonio, she would never regret the choice she and Paul had made.

"Yes, we are. Connected, all of us." She smiled at Ellen. "Thank goodness."

As Kate drove away from Pine Ridge College, she sent up a prayer of gratitude. Not only did she enjoy a number of blessings in her life, but she also had the opportunity to be a blessing to others.

What more could any minister's wife want?

About the Author

BETH PATTILLO is the RITA award-winning author of *Heavens to Betsy* and an ordained minister in the Christian Church (Disciples of Christ). She lives in Nashville, Tennessee, with her husband and two children. Visit her online at www.bethpattillo.com.

Mystery and the Minister's Wife

Through the Fire
by Diane Noble

A State of Grace
by Traci DePree

A Test of Faith
by Carol Cox

The Best Is Yet to Be
by Eve Fisher

Angels Undercover
by Diane Noble

Where There's a Will
by Beth Pattillo